THE JUNIPER HOTEL

Historical Women's Fiction Saga of the Frontier

JUNIPER FALLS
BOOK 1

A.T. BUTLER

JUNIPER FALLS BOOK ONE

THE JUNIPER HOTEL

Historical Women's Fiction Saga

A.T. BUTLER

CHAPTER ONE

"Oh, no . . . no, please. No, surely not. Henry, please tell me this is not what we sold our whole life and took a train almost two thousand miles for."

Charlotte McBride shielded her eyes against the afternoon July sun as she looked up. She stood with her husband and youngest daughter in the dirt on the side of the main street that ran through the center of the frontier town of Juniper Falls, Wyoming Territory. They had been traveling by train for well over a week just to get to this part of the prairie, and then another full day by coach from the train station in Laramie. She had so been looking forward to settling in to her new home, already furnished and comfortable and ready for guests. But now, with the scent of burnt wood filling her nose and the sounds of horses riding by pressing against her ears, she and her husband gazed in horror at the charred face of what until recently had been the General Sherman Inn.

Henry looked down at the papers in his hands and

then back up at the husk of a building. Blackened brick and water-damaged wood and the broken remnants of what furniture had been left inside were all that remained.

"This is it . . . the General Sherman Inn. What could have happened?"

"Oh, I could just cry," Charlotte said.

"It had to have occurred in the last couple weeks," Henry murmured, looking again at his paperwork. "Mr. Bullock at the bank would never have let our loan go through on a burned-down building."

"So, we bought a hotel, and after we put up our several hundreds of dollars, but before we could even arrive to take control of our purchased property, the building burned to the ground? Is that really what you are telling me?"

"Darling, I don't know anything more than you do." Henry sounded exhausted.

Charlotte sighed.

The stagecoach driver who had brought them from the train at Laramie to Juniper Falls stood behind the three McBrides. He cleared his throat. "Do you want— I suppose you don't want me to unload your luggage here, huh, sir?"

Matilda stifled a laugh. How their daughter could find anything to be amused by at a time like this, Charlotte had no idea.

"No, Mr. Cox, please do not. We'll just have to find somewhere else to stay," Henry said, his voice already sounding more firm. Now that the initial shock of their thwarted plans was past, he would find the solution.

"Stay for a bit, if you don't mind. I'm happy to compensate you for your time."

Mr. Cox nodded and stepped back to wait for whatever instructions they would give him.

Charlotte looked around at the other citizens of their new town, passing them on the road or watching from the other storefronts. In the McBrides' plans to come West, they had only corresponded with Mr. Jay Bullock, the bank manager, and Carl Brown, the previous owner of the inn. They had chosen to move all the way out to the frontier, to this town, without knowing anyone here. Charlotte had thought they would have more time to meet their neighbors, time to settle in to this new environment. She had not expected to arrive and immediately need to lean on these strangers for help.

Matilda was looking to her to find them beds for the night. Whatever else had gone wrong, they couldn't sleep in the street. Charlotte and Henry would need to make decisions without any information to go off of, and they would need to do so quickly.

"Well . . ." she said with a resigned sigh. "What do we do now?"

———

Matilda—she preferred Mattie, but her mother refused to remember that—watched as her parents scrambled to decide what they would do next. When they had told her, seven months ago, about their plan to start over again in one of the western territories, her initial reaction had been one of indifference; she had fully expected to be married before her parents left Philadelphia. But when that plan had not played out the way she'd intended, Mattie found herself packing all her worldly possessions into one large trunk, and alighting on the train through Pennsylvania, Ohio, Illinois, until finally arriving in Laramie that morning.

And now, seeing that their proposed home was not even a roof, let alone a building with rooms, Mattie felt vaguely untethered. She was so exhausted from their travel, and from saying goodbye to her beau, that this new situation felt somewhat unreal.

She knew she shouldn't have laughed at the stage-coach driver, but *really*. It was all so . . . ridiculous. For the last several months it seemed to Mattie that anything that could go wrong had. Her own plans had been put on hold indefinitely. What was one more failed intention? Of course the McBrides were homeless. Really, they should have expected as much.

While her parents spoke in low tones about what they would do next, Mattie wandered a few feet away, looking around at her new home.

Though she had left Duncan behind in Philadelphia, she had every reason to believe he would come West after her as soon as he could. He was the only one of the three Shaw siblings to live in that city, and so, when their father's health began to fail, the burden of his care—both physical and of the family business—fell to him. But this meant that he was in no place to marry her, and Mattie was in no place to support herself after her parents left the city, so changes were made. And in the meantime, while she waited for Duncan to follow her

West or send for her to come back East, Mattie would see what there was to see in this western town.

As someone who had lived all her life in one of the oldest and largest cities in the United States, to Mattie the very fact that the main street here was dirt was a curiosity. She had learned from her father that much of the economy of Juniper Falls was ranching; she had never known someone to own more than a couple cows at one time. It was all new and interesting and—once they had a place to stay—she was looking forward to poking around and learning all about what it was like to live way out here in the wilderness. The very fact that it took eight hours to reach a train station was fascinating and strange.

Though, Mattie thought, she should probably keep such judgments to herself. She knew she could be snobby about her city life, and didn't want to alienate potential friends. Instead, she would find all sorts of different and interesting things in this frontier town. It was all new and—for now at least—it was all still exciting.

———

From her spot on the boardwalk outside the general store, Edith Bennett watched the new family as they stood in front of the burned-out shell of the hotel. She had a sack of flour cradled in one arm, and the handle of a full basket looped over the other. Though she had intended to spend her afternoon cleaning the ash out of her fireplace and stove, now Edith was distracted.

She had run her boarding house in Juniper Falls for more than ten years now. For the longest time, her home had been the only option for visitors to stay overnight when visiting. About four years ago, the General Sherman Inn had gone up, across the street from one of the saloons, and Edith had to adjust her life and her business to the change. The city was growing, and more folks needed beds. She always did her best, but Edith knew she could not compete with a hotel that offered room service and a concierge.

Still, she had been just as devastated as the rest of the town when a fire had mysteriously taken the inn, just after Carl Brown had left for his daughter's home back in Ohio. It had been a shock, waking most of Juniper Falls at two in the morning with the emergency.

But more than a shock, it was still a mystery how it had happened.

She turned away from the sight of the strangers and walked the couple blocks back to her home. She was far too old to be able to hold all these groceries for much longer. As she walked, she could not help but think of the woman's face as she looked at the ruined hotel.

On the one hand, though it was just a small part of her, Edith had to admit that she resented that there was a hotel in Juniper Falls at all. Her boarding house would be competition for anyone coming to the town to stay any length of time. As long as the General Sherman Inn had been in business, she and the owner had had an uneasy alliance, neither wanting to outright take any business from the other.

On the other hand . . .

Edith walked up the steps to her front porch. Her

boarding house was situated near the end of the long main street of Juniper Falls, and from her porch she could see much of the bustling and traffic that streamed through the town.

On the other hand, there was now nowhere for this poor new family to stay, now that the inn had been burned down.

There really was no question about what she would do. This would be far from the first time she offered space to a person—or family—in need. It was her business, yes, but it was also her heart.

Her mind made up, Edith set to work putting away her staples before heading back out into the summer afternoon.

———

Lillian Frye stood in the doorway of her husband's hardware store after bringing him a hot lunch. It wasn't every day that she was able to treat him in this way, but as the small schoolhouse was closed for the summer months, she had more time at home than she was used to. Which was why she could dawdle this afternoon and watch the new arrivals, looking lost as they stood outside the burned shell of the hotel.

"We still don't know what happened to the inn?" she asked. "Looks like the new owners just arrived."

"Haven't heard anything," her husband murmured as he restocked the new hammers he'd recently received. "I did see the sheriff over there poking around the other day, though."

The General Sherman Inn had caught fire in the

middle of the night only the previous week. Though there were rumors and suggestions, it was not clear how the fire had started, nor how it had spread so quickly. It was a lucky thing that the barbershop and cafe on either side of the inn only suffered minor damage from sparks landing on the roof. If Abner Reed at the Golden Eagle had not been up late and seen the flames, who knew how much more of Main Street could have been burned.

Mrs. Bullock murmured an apology as she pushed past Lillian in the doorway.

"Oh, I'm in the way!" Lillian exclaimed, returning inside. "You keep an eye on them for me," she told her husband. "I want to know if anything interesting happens, but I don't want to stand here watching like a hawk at a mouse burrow."

Ned laughed. "Not sure I'll see much either, since I've got a store to run."

"Oh, fine." She offered him a playful pout. "Guess I'll have to hear my gossip elsewhere."

"You talking about the new folks who bought the inn?" Mrs. Bullock asked as she picked up a small jar of glue. "My husband says they're from Pennsylvania. The McBrides. A few adult children, maybe four or five? I forget. Anyway, as far as we know, they got on the train to come out here before the inn burned down. No way to know for certain how to get word to them until they showed up." She clicked her tongue and shook her head in sympathy. "Surely don't know what I would do in their shoes."

"Goodness," Lillian murmured, moving again to the doorway to watch.

The mother and daughter were standing perfectly framed by the burnt, skeletal doorway, talking. As she watched, wondering what they could possibly be saying to each other, Lillian felt a pang of pity.

CHAPTER TWO

Charlotte stared at the burned mess of the structure that was supposed to be not only her home but her livelihood. A swell of frustration coursed through her. She was only ever conscientious, only ever prepared for all eventualities. In her mind, she and Henry had done everything right, everything as it was expected to be done; there was no reason they should have to deal with even the smallest inconvenience, let alone this actual tragedy that had left them homeless.

But then, she thought with a sigh, that was not how life worked. As much as she absolutely hated that this was the case, Charlotte had learned often enough in her long life—with five children—that some things would forever be outside of her control. She would need to deal with the consequences of other people's mistakes.

"How did this happen?" she asked her husband again as they stood on the side of the road. "I thought Mr. Brown left the premises weeks ago."

"That's what he told me," Henry insisted. "And I

didn't hear anything otherwise. I don't know any more than you do, I promise. We'll have to find out from the sheriff or Mr. Bullock or someone."

Charlotte mentally added that to the ever-growing list of things that she needed to worry about now that they had arrived in Juniper Falls. It had already been somewhat of an overwhelming list, even assuming they'd have a home waiting for them.

This was now a whole other problem, one so big as to overwhelm her. She felt exhausted. She had just wanted to get to her new home, find something warm to eat, and fall into her new bed under her new roof and sleep until tomorrow.

But that certainly would not be happening any time soon.

Across the street and down a little ways was the town's one saloon, and she was distracted slightly by the raucous laughter and piano playing that floated through the doorway. She looked the other direction, down Main Street, and noticed a sign for a cafe. If it was the kind of place open for supper, they could get food there, probably. Hopefully. Looking up the street again, she wondered where the post office might be, or where else they could learn about where there might be rooms for let.

They hadn't been abandoned in the middle of nowhere, she reminded herself. This was a solvable problem.

"All right," Charlotte said, depleted but firm. "I'm going to let myself be upset about this for another few minutes, and then I suppose we need to find some solutions."

"That's my girl."

Her husband kissed her cheek and went to speak to the stagecoach driver, still waiting for instructions as to what to do with the McBrides' trunks before he could return to the train station.

Charlotte stepped closer to the remains of what had once been the General Sherman Inn, the building in which she had invested all her future and that of her family. The double front door had either burned or been hauled away, and the doorframe stood empty, allowing a clear view to the interior, which was lit by the afternoon sun streaming through. From this vantage, Charlotte could see what used to be a front desk of sorts, and the bulk of a wide, wooden staircase heading up to the second floor, but not much else. The large chandelier had crashed to the floor in the center of the lobby, and the sofas, tables, and chairs that had—presumably—been scattered invitingly were now barely identifiable as furniture. What had probably been a lovely brass pot for a plant looked as though it was covered in charcoal and was lying on its side, soil scattered across what was left of the wooden floor. Everything was black or water-damaged, and Charlotte could not even wrap her mind around where they should start in any kind of repairs.

At that thought, she wondered if Henry would even want to push forward with repairs. Though the McBrides did not have many options, deciding whether or not to go on with their original plans in this new city, or cut their losses and go back East, to where they at least had friends and family, would be the first they would need to consider.

"Smells like a campfire," Matilda said.

Charlotte turned to look at her youngest daughter, standing just behind her and examining the interior of the inn with her.

"Do you see anything worth saving?"

"Not from here. Maybe the fire wasn't as bad on higher floors," Matilda suggested. "But I don't think we should walk up those stairs."

"No, you're right. I suspect we'd fall right through."

"It might not be all bad," Matilda said gently, after a moment. "We could refurbish it exactly the way we want to. New furniture, new wallpaper. We could even move some walls around, maybe. Take the opportunity to reorganize the floor plan."

"Do you know how much that would cost?"

"No," she admitted.

"Well . . ." Charlotte sighed for what felt like the hundredth time. "Your father and I will have to talk about it. It's a big project, to say the least, and maybe this obstacle has changed his mind about all of it."

"You think he'll want to go back to Philadelphia?"

"I'm not sure. All I know is that our plan for this new venture has been turned completely upside down."

"New plan, I suppose," her daughter said. "I'm not worried. This could even be fun."

"I wish I had half your optimism."

Matilda nudged her gently with her shoulder.

"Where's your father?" Charlotte asked, looking around. "Since Mr. Bullock is the only person we have even corresponded with in Juniper Falls, maybe he should go to the bank to speak to him before we do anything else."

"I think we should find a place to stay before we do anything else."

"Well, yes, that would be ideal, but . . . do you want to just walk into the hardware store there"—Charlotte pointed across the street—"and ask whoever you happen to run into?"

Matilda shrugged. "I could."

"All right, ladies," Henry said as he strode to meet his wife and daughter. "Mr. Cox says there is a well-regarded boarding house here, but if that is full there are a few rooms above the saloon, and if all else fails then possibly the pastor's family could find space for us. Seems he and his wife do that for strays now and again."

"Oh, I would hate to impose on the pastor," Charlotte protested. "Seeing as we have no way of knowing how long it will be. And I don't like the idea of Matilda living above the saloon." She shot her daughter a look, but the girl just grinned teasingly. There was no question that she trusted their youngest, but Matilda did like to cause trouble from time to time.

"Maybe it won't come to that," Henry said. "Should we find food first, or locate this boarding house?"

"Excuse me?" a female voice called.

Charlotte turned to look—a woman a bit older than herself, graying hair pulled tightly back and a well-used apron worn over her navy-blue calico dress. The expression on her face was one of reluctant concern, and Charlotte immediately felt badly about arriving in a town full of strangers and needing assistance before even introducing themselves.

"Yes, ma'am. Can I help you?" Henry responded.

The stranger looked from one McBride to another. "I'm sorry. I never do this, but I couldn't help but notice . . . Are you all the new owners of the inn?" she asked with a wince.

"We are," Charlotte said, dejected.

The woman sighed and smiled kindly. "I'm so sorry. I can't imagine what you must be feeling right now, to arrive in town only to find, well . . . this."

"It was a surprise, to say the least," Henry agreed.

"My name is Mrs. Bennett. Edith Bennett. I don't know if you have plans or any idea of what you want to do now, but . . ." She gestured over her shoulder toward the other end of the main street. "I run a boarding house, just down there a ways, and I have a vacant room right now. It might be a bit crowded for all three of you, but we can't have you sleeping on the street." She laughed awkwardly.

"You sure you want to be helping your competition?" Charlotte asked. She was half-joking, but only just. "I'm sure we are all very grateful for the offer. Truthfully, I am too tired right now after so much travel, and then the shock of this news, to be able to think of what to do next. We might have been standing out here lost until midnight if you hadn't said something."

"Well, we can't have that."

The new woman offered her hand to Charlotte, who took it gratefully, letting herself be tucked under Edith's wing and led away from the mess of the shuttered inn.

"Bobby," their new friend said to the stagecoach driver. "You want to bring their things around to my place? I'll get Silas or Jack to help you unload it all."

The man nodded, quickly making his way back to his team and coach while Edith led the McBrides down the dirt road toward the faded gray two-story house near the end of the street.

"I've been here ten years myself," she was telling Charlotte as they walked. "And I'm happy to help you get settled in. Whatever you need. Our businesses may be similar, but neighbors have got to look out for each other, don't you think?"

"Yes, please. Thank you," Charlotte said, full of so much gratitude it made her slightly dizzy. "Meeting you is the first lucky stroke we've had since arriving. One of our trunks got left behind and had to catch up with us in Chicago, and Mr. Cox was late picking us up from the station, and—" Her stomach growled so loudly that Charlotte stopped speaking, embarrassed.

"Let's get you to your new home. It might be temporary, but you're welcome to the space as long as you need. I've got folks who have lived there for almost two years now. Don't you worry about a thing, and we'll get you fed and settled in no time."

Charlotte let herself be taken care of by this new woman—this new friend—and hoped with all her heart that this could be, finally, the solid start for her family's new chapter.

CHAPTER THREE

Mattie followed behind as their new neighbor—Mrs. Bennett—led her mother and father toward the boarding house at the end of the street. Though she had never stayed in such a place herself, Mattie had friends in Philadelphia who lived in various boarding houses. They had always seemed cramped and chaotic to her, so many folks crowded into a small area. And while she'd put up with the tight quarters in exchange for the adventure of staying above a saloon, Mattie knew better than to say anything of the sort to her mother.

But on the other hand, live there long enough and your neighbors who had been strangers eventually become like family. Maybe this shift in the McBrides' plans was just the thing to help them make friends in Juniper Falls more quickly. After leaving behind all of Mattie's older siblings, it felt even more as though they were starting from a deficit here in the new town.

She looked back over her shoulder; the stagecoach driver had led his team farther away, so he could better turn around and head back the other direction. Mattie had noticed that Mrs. Bennett had called him by his first name. Perhaps Juniper Falls was the kind of town where everyone knew everyone else. She'd already noticed how many of the men and women doing their shopping and errands along Main Street smiled and greeted one another, taking their time to say hello.

That had certainly not been the case when they lived in Philadelphia. The population of that city had been closing in on one million people; there were easily fewer than one thousand folks in Juniper Falls and the surrounding ranches.

Back home—back *East*, she corrected herself—there had been a several-city-blocks-wide neighborhood where the McBrides had lived in which they knew their neighbors and local shop owners, but anything past a certain intersection was like a whole other city, different extended families, different groups of immigrants. Mattie wasn't sure which experience she would like better. If nothing else, she was up to the challenge.

She hung back, trailing just near enough to hear that the older folks were talking but not so near as to be able to understand what was being said. Whatever it was, her mother would tell her later. Instead, she used the opportunity to look around her new town. Her new home.

On the walk down the main street of Juniper Falls, they passed not just a saloon, general store, and jail, but also a hardware store, laundry, land claims office, and more. Mattie thought she remembered her father saying the town had been founded just after the war between the states, and it seemed that in the intervening decades the locals had settled in nicely. She tried to imagine what it must have been like twenty years prior—with Indian tribes roaming the plains instead of train tracks—but the sight of so many people and signs of civilization all around her made that difficult even for her overactive imagination.

There were plenty of people out at this time in the afternoon, and Mattie was the recipient of several cautious, but welcoming, smiles. She had only been in Juniper Falls for less than an hour and she was already getting warm smiles from strangers, far more than she'd come to expect during her years in Philadelphia.

Mr. Cox's stagecoach passed them just before the four reached the steps leading up to the porch of Mrs. Bennett's boarding house.

"Follow me," Mrs. Bennett said, as she entered her home. "We'll get you something to snack on while I get one of my boys to help unload your things."

Her parents halted just past the door in the parlor of the boarding house. The curtains had been thrown open, and bright afternoon light illuminated the space. To Mattie's eyes, the furniture and ornamentation was more comfortable than luxurious, but that appealed to her. She would hate to be living in a space where she did not feel as though she could be herself or where she was afraid to even sit.

Mrs. Bennett, who had continued on through to the dining room and kitchen, called for the McBrides to follow her. As they entered the room, Mattie overheard Mrs. Bennett giving instructions to someone. Then a tall, sandy-haired young man passed back out through the dining room, nodded to the McBrides, and headed out the front door.

"Have a seat, please," Mrs. Bennett said, as she set down a tray on the dining room table. "Jack is going to go help Bobby get your things up to your room."

Her parents sat, each taking a glass of lemonade gratefully, but Mattie took the chance to walk slowly around the room, looking at the art and wallpaper that Mrs. Bennett had filled the walls with. There was a sense of home here that she loved, and Mattie realized that even though this had not been the original plan, the chance to spend a few weeks, or longer, living here would be . . . comforting.

It would be just the place to land as they made their way in this new town.

From the dining room, they could hear the men making several trips up and down the stairs, as well as soft thuds from the floor above where they presumably were depositing the luggage. Mattie found herself wondering what the story was with the young man who lived here. If he was a long-term tenant or temporary like herself. How he spent his days. When she might see him again. She heard little of the conversation between the older folks as they sipped their lemonade and ate the sandwiches that had been brought in, but before long, Mrs. Bennett led the three McBrides upstairs, to one of the bedrooms along the hall.

It was large enough to hold a double bed, a wide chest of drawers, and a narrow cot set up in the corner. Mattie winced inwardly at the sight of this last—it was surely where she would be sleeping—but she knew it could not be helped.

"I hope you all will be comfortable," their new land-lady said. "I'll send Daisy up with sheets and blankets for the cot before supper. I wish it could be more comfortable for you all, but please just let me know if there's anything you need. I'll leave you alone to get settled, and see you soon for supper with the others."

When the McBrides were left to themselves, Mattie started poking around in the drawers of the chest. There was a bathroom down the hall, and Mrs. Bennett had left clean towels on the top of the chest, but otherwise there was nothing else in the room.

"We'll make it home," her mother said, looking around at the sparse space. "And it won't be forever."

"I promise to be effusively grateful when we do move into the hotel and I get my own room again," Mattie said fervently, hugging her mother from the side. "Things could be a lot worse, Mama. Don't worry about me."

"I'm going to speak to Mr. Cox a moment, ladies," her father said. "To let him know we're still expecting a few things to be shipped west and see if he can bring it to us."

"And I'm going to go exploring," Mattie announced. "Maybe a letter came from Duncan."

"You think it could have gotten here before you?" her father asked. "Even if he wrote the day we left *and* it got on the same train as us, it's not likely to be here yet."

"You never know." She shrugged. "A walk might be nice anyway."

"Don't be too long," her mother said distractedly. "I might need your help to remember everyone's names. And we really should have supper soon. That sandwich won't last you until tomorrow."

"All right. I'll be back in time for supper."

"Sooner!" her mother called after her.

Mattie ducked out the door before either of her parents could ask anything else of her. Though she knew it would be only a matter of time before she got weighted down with a long list of chores or errands—especially with the rebuilding they would need to do—Mattie wanted to use some of this free time while she had it.

She headed down the dark stairs, into the parlor, and then out again to the front porch. The afternoon was getting on, and the sun was on its way toward the western horizon, exactly the direction Mattie was facing. From this spot near the end of the street, she could see all the way down, more than half a mile, to where the white-washed church steeple stood at the other end.

The tall young man who had been helping Mr. Cox bring in her family's luggage sauntered up the front path toward her. He stopped when they met and grinned at her again.

"Miss McBride, right?" he asked. "Sorry to be forward, but I figure, since we're going to be living down the hall from each other, we're bound to become real familiar."

"Mattie McBride, yes. And, I'm sorry . . . if Mrs. Bennett told us your name I've already forgotten it."

"Jack. Jack Kinsey."

He held out his hand, shaking hers with a strong, confident grip that told her that he wasn't the type to treat girls as breakable dolls. She liked him immediately.

"It's nice to meet you, Jack. I wonder if you could help me with just one other thing?"

"Whatever you like."

"Where's the post office?"

"There's a small office at the back of the general store," Jack told her. "Post office, telegraph, and messenger service locally when needed. If you want to wait a minute, I can show you."

"Oh, thank you, but I think I'd like to explore on my own."

Jack grinned at her again, this time wide enough for a single dimple to flash in his left cheek. "Sounds like an adventure. Have fun. And I hope I'll see you at supper. Mrs. B makes the best chicken pie I've ever had."

"Thank you. I'm looking forward to it."

He tipped his hat to her as he stood aside and let her continue down the path. Mattie was more and more pleased with every interaction she'd had since arriving in Juniper Falls, the burned-down hotel notwithstanding.

Though there was no letter waiting at the post office for her—she didn't really expect there to be—Mattie did get to meet the postmaster and telegraph operator, Mr. Quinn, who made a note of their names and new address at Mrs. Bennett's. She also got to talk to a couple other women who were shopping in the general store at the time, from whom she got a recommendation for Sunshine Cafe, and she witnessed a small quarrel between two men, one of whom was almost certainly drunk.

Juniper Falls was not nearly as rough and wild as she had feared when she first learned they would be moving to a small town on the Wyoming frontier. It was welcoming, and fascinating, and she was looking forward to whatever came next.

CHAPTER FOUR

Edith heard the front door close and wondered who had left. At the moment, in addition to the McBride family, her tenants included Jack Kinsey and Silas Denbow, young bachelors who had both been living there a long time and shared the tiniest room with bunkbeds, as well as Mr. and Mrs. Watkins, and another bachelor named Bill Stuart. Her friend and employee-of-sorts, Daisy, was not exactly a paying tenant, but lived in the small room above the kitchen in exchange for her labor around the place. That left one last small, empty room that sat at the front of the house, over the porch. It was generally the last room that Edith rented out, given the noise from the street that might disturb guests. She was, in fact, thinking about moving into that room herself. With how little sleep she'd been getting lately, maybe it would be better to have her own, larger, room available to guests.

After inserting herself into their conversation in front of the inn, Edith had fed the McBrides, helped them get settled in to their room, and then headed back down to the kitchen. Her afternoon plans of cleaning the ash out of the stove were somewhat delayed, but if she hurried she'd have time before she had to start supper. She stood in the middle of her silent kitchen for a long moment, thinking, rearranging plans, and stretching recipes to accommodate three new people.

"All right, Edith," she muttered to herself. "Now's the time to focus and get it all done."

She had been planning to make chicken pot pies for supper that night, but that meant that she needed to make up the dough for the crust as soon as possible. It would still need time to rest and then also be baked through before the ravenous young men who looked to her for room and board came home hungry. Always hungry, those ones.

Edith rolled up the cuffs of her sleeves and got to work.

More than an hour later, she had finished the pie crust and let it sit while she roasted the vegetables that would make up much of the dish's filling. The meat would come from the roast chicken she had made the previous day, mixed in with the vegetables and thickened broth that she still needed to finish. As she brushed off loose strands of hair that had stuck to her damp brow, she thought that maybe tomorrow she'd make a cold chicken salad. It was far too hot in July to keep the fire in the oven stoked all day.

Edith was wiping her hands on her apron and looking around her kitchen, trying to remember what else she wanted to finish before supper, when someone interrupted her. She looked up to see Daisy entering the kitchen through the back door, her arms full of firewood.

"Did you get all that chopped today?" she asked, surprised. "Thank you so much. I've got to make supper for three extra guests now, and was wondering if there was enough fuel to cook all of that tonight."

"New people?" Daisy said as she carefully stacked the wood in the pile next to the stove.

"As a matter of fact . . ." Edith turned to her friend. "A couple and their daughter. The new owners of the General Sherman Inn, actually."

"No!" Daisy gasped, her eyes wide. "Oh, those poor things."

Edith nodded. "And it was as we suspected—they had no idea of the damage before they showed up here with all their trunks and luggage."

Daisy shook her head. "Well, at least you had the room available for them. I suppose it could have been worse. I can't imagine. If you hadn't taken me in when I showed up . . ."

"It could have been so much worse, you're right, but still. Just think about what they're all up against now. Starting over with nothing like what they had expected. No friends yet, no other family. The best thing we can do is at least make their living situation easy in the meantime."

"What else do you need me to do right now?"

"Oh, thank you! I had just been standing here wondering what I had forgotten when you walked in, actually. I told the family—the McBrides—that you would bring them sheets and things. Their daughter, maybe eighteen years old, is crowded in there on the cot with them. They have clean towels, but could you dress the bed for them, please?"

"Of course," Daisy replied genially. "I'll just wash this sawdust off my hands and get right to it."

Edith sighed gratefully. "I honestly don't know what I would do without you."

Daisy beamed at her before heading toward the staircase up to her room.

As she listened to the footsteps climbing up, Edith reflected that she truly could not remember how she had gotten everything done before Daisy had arrived. The poor woman had escaped an abusive husband and somehow stumbled onto Edith's front porch in a state of exhaustion and hunger about a year earlier. When it had eventually been discovered that Daisy's husband had died in the week since she had gotten free, Edith offered her a room in her boarding house, and the younger woman had been here ever since.

They were a well-matched team, patient and kind with each other even while living side by side. Each tried to give the other whatever space she needed while at the same time feeling safe to ask for help. After her husband died, Edith had run the boarding house on her own for ten years. While she would have gone looking for more help eventually, she was grateful every day for the friendship and support that had so unexpectedly shown up on her doorstep.

Although Daisy had never asked for more than the roof over her head and food to eat, Edith wondered if there was something more she could offer the other woman who had added so much to her life.

As she checked on the status of the roasting vegetables, she was still wondering what Daisy might want or need, when Bill Stuart burst into the kitchen, looking around wildly. She had missed him at supper the night before, and had heard him come in late. He was tall and thin, with limbs that seemed too long for even his height. His hair badly needed washing, and his mustache looked to be stained by tobacco.

Edith froze. This man had been living in her boarding house for seven months, since he had first arrived in Juniper Falls, nearly penniless and clearly running from something in his past. He had always been polite, had always paid his rent on time, but there was something about his manner—both now and several times in the past—that felt unsafe. It was as though he could not quite be trusted to control his impulses; Edith did not know him well enough to trust that those impulses would be harmless. He had been a captain in the Confederate Army nearly twenty years earlier, but still insisted he be addressed by that now-defunct title.

"Captain Stuart," she said finally, when he did not supply an explanation for his manner. "Is there something you need? Since you weren't here for supper last night, I'm happy to fix you something now."

"New people, aren't there?"

"Excuse me?" Edith's surprise at seeing him was hindering her ability to parse what he was saying.

"That's what Jack told me. You all got new people in here. A family, he said. Who are they?"

Edith thought quickly, wondering what this poor man might be going through that he had discarded all previous politeness. "A couple and their grown daughter, here from Philadelphia. They are the new owners of the inn, but since it's not fit to live in . . ."

Bill was pacing a circle around the kitchen, looking more agitated than Edith had ever seen him—more even than the day he'd arrived.

"Captain Stuart, is there something I can do for you? You seem . . ."

His eyes flashed to her as her sentence trailed off.

"Nothing," he said finally, letting out a long breath. "It's nothing. It's fine. It's nothing. I need to . . . I need to go see someone. I don't know if I'll be back for supper."

"All right—"

But he had already gone.

Edith remained frozen, watching the doorway where he had disappeared. One of these days, she realized, she might have to ask him to leave. She could not stand being unsettled like this in her own home for much longer. Perhaps now, with the McBrides staying here, she could afford to let another room sit empty for a bit.

With a sigh—finances, time, energy, and her other limited resources weighing on her, always weighing on her—Edith turned back to her oven. Realizing she would not have a chance to clean out the ashes now, while she waited for the vegetables to be done roasting, she started working on her list of chores that would need to be completed tomorrow.

CHAPTER FIVE

Lillian left her husband's hardware store and walked slowly back home. In the time that she had been speaking to him, it seemed as though the new family had dispersed, likely finding a last-minute place to stay at Mrs. Bennett's.

Lillian could not imagine how stressful it must be for them to arrive in Juniper Falls and have everything they had expected to find just . . . gone. Literally turned to ash.

But she was glad they'd found someplace to go out of the sun and the street. And since there was nothing more for her to watch, there was no longer a good reason for Lillian to stay in the street or in the store.

There were always chores for her to do at home.

Maybe she could find out where the new family was staying—most certainly at Edith's now, but also long term—and make herself useful. Showing them around town. Even helping with the inn in some way, if they were determined to recoup their losses there.

There was still a month left of her summer vacation, and Lillian was running out of things to occupy her time before the school year started again.

She knew what Ned would say about that. She could hear him now:

"Don't you think you should be resting, my dear? Most women take months or years to grieve. Maybe sticking closer to home would be best, nesting or sewing or taking care of yourself instead of other people."

Lillian strolled slowly down the side streets to their small home a couple blocks north of the main street of Juniper Falls. She and her husband and younger sister had come West from Baltimore just about a year earlier. Though it had not been her first choice, when she and Ned married she'd promised him that she would follow him West as long as she could continue to teach in whatever town they had ended up in. He had been reluctant —no married women were schoolteachers anywhere near where they'd lived—but in the end, his confidence in the opportunities that the territories allowed outweighed his concern.

Lillian's younger sister, Mary Ann, had come with them, and here in Juniper Falls Ned had found the perfect place to follow his dream of owning his own store, his own land, and building a home for their future. The crowded neighborhoods and prices back in Baltimore would have made such a venture nearly impossible, but here on the Great Plains, Lillian got to watch her husband thrive.

She reached the street in front of her own house— lovely pale green sideboard with white trim. It was far nicer and cozier than she ever would have dreamt of if they'd stayed in Baltimore. Lillian felt a surge of gratitude for her husband. She noticed that Mary Ann was working in the garden. They had planted vegetables in the sunny patch behind the house a few months earlier, but Mary Ann had insisted on decorative flowers here in front.

"You're later than I expected," she said, as she stood and wiped the dirt from her hands onto her apron. "Did something happen?"

"Not to me, thankfully," Lillian told her sister, before going on to explain, in great detail, the new family she had seen outside of the burned-down hotel. "It just makes me so grateful for what we have," she concluded. "I can't imagine how upset they must be. Remember how difficult the transition was when *we* first got here?"

All while Lillian had been talking, Mary Ann had been clipping some of the larger blossoms and putting together a small bouquet, her hand getting fuller and fuller with each bloom.

"Do you want to come inside with me to finish your story?" she asked Lillian. "I'd like to put these in water."

"Oh, there's not more to say." She followed Mary Ann into the house, both removing their hats as they stepped across the threshold. "But I was thinking about if it would be better to call on them at Mrs. Bennett's and offer help, or if they might better need time and space to settle in. I don't want to overwhelm them when they have so much already to attend to. But, then again, perhaps now is when they'll need my help most . . ."

The family's front sitting room was small, while still being full of bright natural light from the big front window. Whatever scuffs or boot marks that had marred the floorboards were hidden beneath a braided rag rug. Mary Ann always kept the wooden side tables polished and gleaming, and Lillian breathed in the faint lemon scent. Against the far wall stood a horsehair-stuffed settee, draped with a crocheted afghan in cheerful yellows and blues.

Mary Ann returned to the sitting room with a water-filled vase, arranging the flowers in a vase for the table closest to the settee.

"But then," Lillian continued, somewhat self-consciously, "I don't know how much I could do for them anyway. It's not as though I will be able to build them a new front door or rebuild the staircase . . . and Mrs. Bennett is quite capable herself, surely she has already supplied them with all the home comforts they might need for now . . ."

"I think maybe you're ready to go back to school," Mary Ann finally said with a laugh. "Once you're with those children for so many hours each day, you won't have the time or energy to think through seventeen possible different responses to a new family arriving in town."

"Goodness! You're right." Lillian sank into one of the chairs. "By June I'm always thrilled for it to be summer so I can have my break, but then, now, by the time the end of July rolls around, I have had quite enough, thank you very much."

"When you have children of your own at home you'll never be bored."

Lillian smiled tightly. That was precisely another reason—maybe *the* reason, truthfully—that she did not want to just stay at home this summer. It may be the last time that she had hours of time just to herself.

"I need help making supper if you need something to do," Mary Ann continued.

"Yes, please. Help me keep my hands busy."

The two sisters worked together over the afternoon, while Lillian put the new family out of her mind. No matter anything else, there wasn't a thing she could do for them at that minute.

Within a few hours, supper was finished and on the table, just on time for Ned to return after his long day at the store. Lillian was setting the table for the three of them when she heard him come in and hang up his coat and hat.

"How was the rest of your afternoon?" she called. "What happened?"

"Easy." He entered, kissed her cheek, and found his seat at the head of the table. Lillian watched as her husband leaned back in his chair, stretching. "Just enough customers to keep me occupied, but nothing difficult. These flowers are lovely. Are they from our garden?"

"Mary Ann picked them. But," she continued doggedly, "you didn't see that new family again?"

"I wasn't standing by the door watching, honey, no. Why are you so interested in them?"

"Oh, I don't know . . . Something to do, I suppose. I'm just curious."

At that moment Mary Ann brought in the fresh bread and a cold lettuce salad, setting them within reach of Ned on the dining room table. "Can you help me with the rest, sister?"

Lillian followed her back to the kitchen, and returned following behind her with chicken noodle soup and berries with cream to round out the meal. Summer was her favorite season, not just because she had days away from the schoolhouse. The fresh produce to which the family had access, now that they were no longer living in a big city, was heaven-sent.

Finally, she sat down. She had not realized how hungry she was until the scent of the warm chicken broth reached her nostrils.

"Goodness, Mary Ann, where did you learn to be such a good cook?"

"The same place you did, sister, dear. Ma had me in the kitchen as soon as I could be trusted with a knife."

"And yet somehow you never manage to leave bones in the broth or burn the bottoms of pans the way I do."

"Just one of God's favorites, I suppose," Mary Ann said teasingly.

"Silas Denbow is a very lucky man," Ned interjected.

Mary Ann blushed. "Stop!"

"He's been courting you long enough now. Surely he'll be asking for your hand any day."

"I don't know anything about that," Mary Ann mumbled as she took her own seat.

Lillian shot her husband a look, silently pleading with him to stop teasing her sister. He waggled his eyebrows at her, but seemed to take the hint, as he only said, "I'll say grace."

Later, when all three had been served and they were digging in to the soup, Ned turned to his wife. "And how did you spend the rest of your afternoon?"

"Mary Ann put me to work. I chopped the potatoes,

washed the lettuce, and a few other things." Lillian gestured to the dishes spread out over the table. "It was all her though. She was just giving me the easy tasks to occupy my time. Honestly, Ned, it seems like every summer I want my break from school to be shorter and shorter. I would bring the children back tomorrow if I could."

He frowned. "But how are you feeling? Surely you're not ready for such exertion."

"I feel like I am," she insisted. "This is another reason why I was thinking I might call on that new family that came to run the hotel. They must need so much help, and I have so much time available to me."

"Yes, but the doctor wanted you to rest during these months, remember?"

Lillian looked down at her plate to hide the tears that suddenly welled up in her eyes. When she had lost their unborn baby a few months earlier, she had tried to explain to Ned how it made her feel. She had tried to show him the way her grief over the loss of their potential family was showing up, but she was not sure he had heard her. He seemed to expect Lillian to spend all day in bed instead of putting the loss behind them and looking forward toward their future.

The fact that she had enough energy to even leave the house seemed surprising to Ned, and on top of that, Lillian's desire to get back to work seemed almost to offend him.

"I have rested," she said, finally looking up at him. "I *do* rest. I get so much sleep every night, and Mary Ann does so much of the housework there's barely any need for me. If she asks me to dust, it's the most I do in a week. But those children—they need me. I can do really good work at school, and I just wish I could go back sooner."

"I thought we had talked about you not going back to work in the fall?" he said gently. "Didn't you tell me you would think about resigning?"

"I did think about it. I have been thinking about it. And if . . ." Her voice cracked. "If we had not lost the baby, I would obviously not be continuing at the school. But we did. We *did*. And . . . and I need the distraction, Ned. I can't just wait around at home, dusting and sitting and waiting anxiously every day for another baby to come along."

"There must be something more to do than dusting." He smiled and glanced at Mary Ann. "Especially after Mary Ann marries her rancher."

While her sister took another bite and refused to acknowledge him, Lillian looked at her husband for a long moment, unsure how to respond. It was clear that she was not going to change his mind about anything over this short dinner conversation, but with the way he was so confident, she was beginning to despair over being able to change his mind at all.

"There are still a few weeks before school starts," he said. "We can talk about it again before then."

Lillian stifled her sigh of frustration, as Mary Ann changed the topic of conversation to the upcoming vegetable harvest. She listened as her sister went on about all the jars and things she would need for canning. Their tomato plants were delivering far more than expected.

Most days Ned was as good of a man and as

supportive of a husband as she could have dreamed about. The very fact that Lillian continuing to work after getting married was not a bigger argument was testament to that.

But even the best men had limits, and she feared she was reaching his.

CHAPTER SIX

The main topic of conversation over the McBride family's first supper at the boarding house was that of Charlotte and Henry. They sat cautiously with these new friends and neighbors, wondering if their landlady had mentioned anything about their dilemma or how much they might have to introduce themselves. Surely everyone in Juniper Falls had heard about the inn burning down.

The McBrides needn't have worried, however. The outpouring of sympathy and assistance the others offered was both surprising and welcome.

Charlotte sat near the foot of the table, with Henry to her right and Matilda to her left, and listened as idea after idea were lobbed their way. Names of laborers they could hire, advice for ordering furniture to be shipped out from the eastern states, ideas for what kind of amenities the hotel could offer guests in time, tales about seasonal festivals they could look forward to.

It was so much to be thinking about, but at least

Charlotte was not also expected to uphold her end of the conversation. While they sat at supper with new friends, all talking over the McBrides' problems and offering solutions, she had felt grateful, yes, but also overwhelmed. At one point during the meal, Charlotte felt as though she was missing much of what was being said, with such a glut of advice as they were being given.

After supper, she and Henry made their polite excuses so that they could return to the peace of their private room, and Charlotte fell asleep blessedly early, despite the new surroundings and the less-than-quiet boys living down the hall.

The next day, in the light of a new morning, Charlotte and Henry had a list as long as her arm of things they needed to get done, and all of them seemed to need doing as soon as possible. But at least now, after the previous night's conversation, they had some idea of where to begin and who to ask. When she woke—before dawn, since she had fallen asleep so early—she readied herself for the day as quietly as she could so as not to wake the rest of her family, and headed down to the first floor of the boarding house. Henry woke as she was pinning up her hair, and was not far behind her, leaving Matilda to sleep as best she could in the small cot.

"Good morning," her husband murmured to Charlotte when she met him at the foot of the stairs. "I'm not sure Mattie slept much, but you seemed to. I don't know the last time I heard you snore."

"I felt as though I was dead to the world," Charlotte said. "I didn't realize quite how tired I was until we left the supper table."

"Not every day will be as long and as hard as yesterday was."

"Goodness, let's hope."

She led the way into the dining room, where the morning sun was just beginning to stream through the large window at the back of the house. Despite the early hour, the room was not empty. One of the young men—Silas, Charlotte thought his name was—sat hunched over his plate, sopping up egg yolk with a piece of toast. When the McBrides entered, he grinned at them, acknowledging them as best he could without speaking through a mouth full of food.

"Good morning," Henry said. "Should we . . . get breakfast from the kitchen, or . . . ?"

Daisy walked in at that moment with a plate in each hand. "Sit, sit. I heard you coming. I won't always be this prompt, but we try to keep things easy here for break-fast." She placed a plate in front of each of them as she continued. "Utensils are there in the center of the table. I'll be right back with coffee. Excuse me."

Silas had swallowed by then, and gestured to the empty seats across from him. "Sit! You folks sleep all right? I know Jack and me can sound like wild horses up and down that hallway sometimes."

"I slept very well," Charlotte said, politely declining to comment on the young man's noisiness. "And really, we are so grateful to have a place to sleep at all, after everything."

"I bet." Silas stood, picking up his cleaned plate and empty coffee mug. "I've got to be heading out to the ranch, but I'm sure I'll see you all later. Hope you get to everything you want to. Good luck."

As he exited toward the kitchen, Daisy entered carrying a tray. Several mugs, cream, sugar, and a carafe of coffee that Charlotte fancied she could smell from a dozen feet away.

"And there's more where all of this comes from," Daisy said, as she set the tray in front of the McBrides. "I'm sorry to run, but Edith needs me. You all holler if you need something else."

And with that, Charlotte and Henry were left alone with their breakfast. It was an appreciated change of pace after last night's warm but overwhelming reception. As her husband poured her coffee, she looked down at her breakfast—two fried eggs, two slices of toast with butter, a fat slice of ham, and diced, roasted potatoes seasoned with what smelled like garlic. She thought she had eaten plenty the night before, but was easily hungry again after looking at this spread. If these were the kinds of hearty meals that were included with the price of the room here, Charlotte wondered how Mrs. Bennett could possibly be making much of a profit.

It was exactly the kind of predicament Charlotte knew was waiting for them when they—*if* they—opened their inn. She put these thoughts from her mind as her husband spoke.

"This all smells so amazing," Henry said, as he cut into his ham. "We won't be hungry for hours after this."

"And that's a good thing." Charlotte followed her husband, tasting a small bite of the ham as she talked. "We have a lot to do today."

"Where did you want to start? We can go talk to Mr. Chandler, like Mr. Watkins suggested. We could just hire a handful of boys to clean up the space. We could get a meeting with Mr. Bullock and talk about the financial investment and what our options are." He paused, peered into her face. "We could go back to bed and sleep for a week, worry about all of this later."

"Stop." She put her hand up, overwhelmed again by all the decisions that needed to be made. "I don't know . . . I need to think. I suppose I'm grateful that all these considerations did not keep me awake last night, but I need a little more time to think through all of it."

Henry ate silently, giving her the quiet she needed while she tried to focus.

"All right." She nodded to herself as she pushed her potatoes around her plate. "All right, we can figure this out. We're both smart, capable people."

"One of us more than the other," Henry interjected with a wink.

Charlotte laughed, despite all the stress and worry. There was no doubt that over the several decades of their marriage she had been the one to make sure everything in their life ran smoothly, and she appreciated the acknowledgment.

"Are you worried?" he asked more gently.

They had not really been alone in . . . Charlotte thought back. Weeks? At least. Even the previous night, their daughter had been in the room with them. She knew that her husband worried about her, and she saw his question for what it was: checking in to see what he could do for her; an offer to take on some of her worry. The hotel and the money would all figure themselves out eventually, but Henry was taking the time, here, now, to ensure that his wife was happy—or at least all right.

"I'm not worried," she said. "I'm just . . . expecting to be very tired for the next month."

"Ah, well, that would have been true even if the hotel had been pristine."

"Goodness, I'm sure you're right." She sighed.

Their landlady, Mrs. Bennett, entered from the kitchen just then. "I'm sorry, I hope I'm not interrupting, but I wanted to give you this before you all left for the day."

She didn't sit, but stood behind one of the chairs on the other side of the table, withdrew a folded piece of paper from the pocket of her apron, and slid it across the damask tablecloth to Henry.

"It's directions for where to find Mr. Chandler, and also the bank. If he's not at home, he's likely finishing up the Watkinses' house. Everyone in town is quite approachable, and I don't doubt you'll have any trouble, but just in case."

"Thank you." Henry glanced at the paper before sticking it in his coat pocket. "We're just so thrilled with how generous everyone here seems to be. We've been made to feel most welcome."

"I don't know what I had expected before we came here," Charlotte said. "Outlaws, maybe?" She chuckled. "But this is so much better than I could have dreamed."

Mrs. Bennett nodded. "I know Daisy told you the same, but please just let us know if you need something. I want this to feel like home." She looked up, distracted; Charlotte heard it too—those horses Silas had mentioned. "I think I hear someone else above, so I'm going to hustle back to make up their breakfast."

Though she had not expected to be so quickly thrust

into such intimate quarters with strangers, Charlotte had to acknowledge that such a plunge could work out for the best. They had, after all, made half a dozen friends in just their first day in Juniper Falls. Now, as they were about to go out to try to find solutions to their biggest obstacle, they'd already received more unlooked-for assistance. And they hadn't even finished breakfast.

Footsteps sounded down the staircase, and a moment after their landlady had left, Mr. and Mrs. Watkins entered the dining room. They sat across the table, reaching for the empty coffee mugs and carafe.

"Morning, McBrides," the husband said. "Hope you're getting ready for your big day."

Charlotte glanced at her own husband. Nothing had been decided, and now their moment to be alone was over. The stress of all the pieces was already wearing on her.

"Enjoy your breakfast," Henry told her, nodding at the plate which Charlotte had barely touched. "There's time for all of this, but you can't do it without food in your belly."

She smiled at him, grateful, and cut herself a much bigger bite of ham.

CHAPTER SEVEN

When the McBrides had expected to arrive in Juniper Falls to a working hotel, it was assumed that Mattie would take on the role of chambermaid, or occasional hostess, alongside her mother. With the enormous change of plans, however, she was left with no clear direction or idea about how to help. She was rudderless in a town where she knew no one, and she'd never been very good at entertaining herself.

Mattie was still waking up in her narrow cot in the corner of their boarding house room when her parents had gotten dressed for the day and left. Though she knew she would—likely, hopefully—get used to it, sleeping this first night in a new bed, a new place, was frustrating. Mattie had tossed and turned all night, and the very fact that her parents had allowed her to loll about in bed for so long told her that they must have noticed how poorly she'd been sleeping on the train for the previous week.

There was so much to do, and though Mattie did not

know what precisely her tasks would be to ready the hotel for guests—a concept that, on this bleary morning, felt far out of reach—she did not think she would be afforded many more mornings like this.

She yawned, and stretched to sitting, the light blanket pooling about her waist.

They had arrived in Juniper Falls in what was likely the hottest part of the year. July had a few more days, and then August, and then still several more weeks before true autumn weather arrived. While cleaning and managing guests in such heat would have been bad enough, having to do any kind of construction and difficult manual labor would be downright awful.

Mattie was not looking forward to it, though perhaps they would get more of a breeze out here on the prairie, with all the wide-open space, so different from the narrow streets of Philadelphia. She wondered if she had enough money saved to buy herself a new dress, since she surely would be sweating through the few she had quickly.

She could hear other people moving about the boarding house: the murmurs of conversations, a door closing down the hall somewhere. There was no clock that she could see from her cot, but she didn't think Mrs. Bennett would hold breakfast forever.

Besides, it might be cooler downstairs.

Mattie dressed, pinned up her hair, and headed down the staircase toward the sounds of conversation and clinking tableware. She found her parents still seated at the breakfast table, though the plates in front of them were empty. Daisy sat with them, and all three seemed deeply engaged with whatever they had been talking about.

As Mattie entered, Daisy jumped to her feet. "I've been saving you a plate! I think it's still warm. Have a seat and I'll be right back."

She practically ran to the kitchen as Mattie sat gratefully. She couldn't help another yawn, however, and her mother, seeing this, poured her a cup of steaming coffee.

"I'm sorry, sweetheart," she said, pushing the full mug over to her daughter. "I know that cot can't be the most comfortable place to sleep."

Mattie shrugged and yawned again. "What are we doing today?"

"We were just discussing that," her father answered. "Got sidetracked a bit when the Watkinses were eating breakfast with us, but now I think we've got it. The first thing your mother and I need to do is talk to Mr. Bullock and find out if the state of the business has affected our loan or access to funds in any way. We can't very well move forward until we know what we have to spend."

"I hate the idea of spending any more . . ." her mother said. "But hopefully Mr. Bullock can give us workable options."

Daisy returned with a plate piled high with a warm, hearty breakfast. Eggs, potatoes—truthfully Mattie didn't much care what it was, she was that hungry.

"Thank you!" She accepted the plate eagerly and immediately took a big bite of toast, then said to her parents, her mouth full, "So what do you need me to do?"

Daisy, smiling at her appetite, left the room.

"Nothing yet," her mother said wearily. "I don't know yet. There's just so many things to do—"

"Can I go to the hotel?"

Her mother frowned. "There's nothing *at* the hotel."

"Actually—" Mattie chewed quickly and swallowed. "Actually, there's a *lot* at the hotel. I don't know how closely you looked inside, but the interior is still a mess. I don't think anyone has actually gone *in* there. Lumber and broken furniture everywhere. I was thinking I could at least . . . I don't know. Move some of that stuff? Even if it's just dragging the garbage close to the door so someone else can haul it away?"

"You really want to spend your day like that?" her mother asked dubiously. "Sounds very difficult. Hot. Exhausting."

"It won't hurt me. I'll be careful of splinters, and I won't work myself too hard. I don't really know how else I can help at this stage. Do you? I could sit in the parlor and knit, I suppose."

"It's not that . . . I just worry . . . A young woman, on her own, trying to move heavy things . . . What will the neighbors say?"

Mattie held her tongue—made easier by the fact that she had just taken another huge bite of her breakfast. She had learned long ago that her mother's first instinct was to please everyone around her, but if she let her mother think a situation all the way through she would always come to the more reasonable, practical position. There was nothing inherently wrong or inappropriate with Mattie doing such labor in a public place in the middle of the day. And anyone who would have a problem with it was not the kind of person she cared to cater to.

That was not a sentiment she would ever talk her mother into, though.

While she ate, she watched the small expressions shift over her mother's face, and she noticed the exact moment she came to the same conclusion Mattie had: the work needed to be done, and it wouldn't really hurt anything or anyone if Mattie was the one to start it.

"I don't know how much I can get done by myself," Mattie added, "but it's something. Better than me wasting time looking at wallpaper samples we can't use yet."

"Oh, I don't know," her mother replied with an indulgent smile. "Who knows how long it will take to get those wallpaper orders shipped from Boston. Maybe the sooner the better."

"Mama . . ." Mattie groaned.

"You would really rather move broken furniture around than think about how we are going to decorate?" her father asked.

"Like you wouldn't believe."

He chuckled. "It's fine by me then."

Mattie resumed her eating as her parents exchanged a communicative look, but she knew she had won. Accordingly, once she had cleaned her plate—she felt full enough to not need another meal until supper—she borrowed a canteen of water from Mrs. Bennett and left the boarding house the same time as her parents. With the boarding house at one end of the long main street, it was easy for Mattie to get her bearings and find her way back to the hotel, just a few blocks away. Her parents continued on to the bank, which was farther toward the other end of the street, leaving her alone for the day.

The scent of charred wood greeted her, as it had the day before, and she wondered how long it would take for that smell to dissipate. It didn't appear to have rained at all since the hotel had originally burned down, but maybe with time they would not be reminded of the fire every time they looked at the building.

She stood just outside the front door for the second time in as many days, looking in and trying to assess where she should even start. Some of the bigger pieces would need to stay where they were for now—she was only one person, after all. And she shouldn't try to go up to the second level yet, of course. But there could be some sense made out of the chaos.

Mattie was already looking forward to whatever satisfaction she'd feel at the end of the day. There was nothing she enjoyed more than visible, tangible evidence of her efforts.

"Can I help you, miss?" came a gruff voice behind her.

She turned to see a man approaching her, young around the eyes but older than her, who seemed to be hiding behind his thick, dark beard. He wore a faded brown duster and a wide-brimmed hat, and on his chest he sported a shiny lawman's badge.

"I've got to ask you to not meddle with this mess. We're still waiting for the owners to come take over the property," he continued. "I imagine they'll tear it down or rebuild."

"Oh, that's me. That is, my parents are the owners. We arrived in town yesterday."

He looked surprised only for a moment, before tipping his hat to her. "Pleasure to meet you, then, Miss . . . ?"

"McBride. Mattie McBride. And you must be the sheriff, here?" She indicated the shiny star on his chest.

"Deputy Inglis. The sheriff is sending a telegram right now, I believe. I'm sorry to have interrupted you, but I wouldn't want to see you hurt yourself. I'm not sure how stable that second floor is."

"Did the sheriff—and you—did you all do any investigation? Do we know how the fire started?"

He pursed his lips, looking thoughtful. "We have some ideas. Nothing certain though. I believe Sheriff Sands is still chasing down some leads, asking some questions."

That was a lot of words to say nothing much substantial, Mattie thought.

"Well . . . is there any objection to me moving things around in there?" She gestured through the empty doorframe into the hotel.

"Only the concern that you might get hurt. You sure you don't want to wait and just let whatever men your daddy hires to do it?"

Mattie felt a flash of temper that she immediately quelled. This man was a stranger to her, and it wasn't his fault if he was used to fragile women who had been raised to be helpless. Instead of saying as much to him, she offered him her most winning smile.

"I greatly appreciate the worry, Deputy, but I won't be doing anything too dangerous. There's not much I can help my parents with, as the business is in this current state, but I can move some of the detritus and broken bits into one big pile to make it easier for someone else in the coming days."

He was nodding, listening, seeming as though he wanted to object again, but Mattie just sailed on.

"I'll tell my parents you all are investigating, though. Thank you so much!"

With a final pleasant smile at the deputy, Mattie turned and entered the dark, smoky interior of what had once been a hotel lobby. She could feel the man watching her for a few moments, but thankfully he turned and left her alone to her work.

She suspected this would not be the last time one of their new neighbors questioned what Mattie was doing.

CHAPTER EIGHT

Charlotte followed her husband into the bank of Juniper Falls. Business was slower than she might have expected; but then, it was still midmorning, and whatever deposits other stores might have would probably not be made until later in the day. She looked around the space, taking in everything, while Henry led them deeper into the room.

Upon entering the Juniper Falls Savings & Loan, Charlotte first noticed the four desks set up in a row heading back along the right side of the big room, culminating in a windowed office in the back corner. Three of those desks were occupied—middle-aged men wearing crisp suits and studious expressions—and all were covered in some pattern of ledgers and loose paper.

On the right side of the room, near the front, was the hint of a staircase going down to a basement level, but it was behind a railing, stopping anyone from wandering down there accidentally. The rest of the open space in the middle of the room was worn, wide, dusty planks, scuffed from years of boots stomping across it. The wooden floor was bare, without even a rug at the entrance, except for the occasional spittoon. But when Charlotte lifted her gaze, she noticed the large, glass chandelier in the center of the high ceiling that must be one of the most luxurious pieces in all of this frontier town.

Parallel to the left wall was a long marble counter, behind which six clerks worked, helping clients make deposits, withdraw cash, or answer questions. The metal grate above the counter protected the clerks in the event of a robbery of some kind, but to Charlotte's eye it seemed just as intimidating to those behind it. She certainly would not want to work behind a wall made to feel like a jail cell.

She slipped her hand into her husband's and followed him farther into the bank, toward the corner office near the back. Though this was not the only time she had been inside a financial institution like this, Henry had always before handled what needed to be handled for them. She felt out of place, and resolved to stay quiet and listen throughout whatever conversation they needed to have with the bank's manager.

At the very least, she did not want to let her worry distract her.

As they drew nearer, from within his office the bank manager seemed to hear them coming. The rotund man looked up at their approach, beaming hopefully. When they reached the doorway, he stood.

As he came around his desk to meet them, he extended his hand and said, "Please tell me that I am correct in my guess that you are Mr. and Mrs. Henry

McBride? I pride myself on knowing just about every face that comes through this town, and since yours are new to me, perhaps you are who I've been expecting? Please, have a seat."

As they sat in the two chairs opposite him, Charlotte felt herself calm slightly in this man's presence. In just a couple short sentences, he somehow had made her feel as though everything was going to be all right.

"I wanted to start," Henry was saying, "by thanking you for all your assistance in helping us get out here at all, Mr. Bullock. We would have been lost without you."

"Say no more." He leaned back in his chair, resting his hands on his stomach complacently. "Favorite part of the job, to be honest. The people part. It's good to see you've gotten here safely. Have you . . ." He leaned forward then, looking at Charlotte across the desk with an expression of concern. "Have you seen the inn, then?"

The McBrides nodded.

"I'm real sorry about that," the banker went on. "If there'd been a way to warn you before you got here, I'd a-done it gladly. But! It's not all bad news."

"Oh, that is such a relief," Charlotte said, almost under her breath.

"We'll get this all sorted. You have my word. But first things first. Did you find a place to stay? I wasn't sure if Mrs. Bennett would have space, but if not—"

"Actually," Henry said, "Mrs. Bennett approached us in the street to ensure we were taken care of. It was surprisingly kind of her, seeing as we may be competing for the same guests in time."

Mr. Bullock was nodding. "Doesn't surprise me at all, not at all. You and she will get along well. Good. Well, if that's settled then, McBrides, I have good news for you. Great news, in fact. So great that you'll want to invite me over for supper. So great, you'll want to name the hotel after me."

Henry laughed, a chuckle Charlotte recognized as uncertain, though she wasn't sure the bank manager would pick up on that. She was afraid Mr. Bullock's words carried the self-congratulatory air of someone who might be trying to take advantage of them, though she wanted so badly to be able to trust him.

"What's that, then?" Henry asked. "We're already quite grateful for all your help so far."

"It's this . . ." The bank manager paused, looking from Henry to Charlotte and back again. "As soon as we got your wire to finalize the sale, I took the liberty of taking out insurance on the building for you. Now, we'll have to talk about what that initial investment cost, as well as any additional amount and other details, but I do believe the paperwork was filed and accepted *before* the fire happened."

Charlotte gasped. "Oh! Oh, Mr. Bullock, you did that for us? I could just cry . . ."

"Now, now, we don't want any of that, dear." He reached across the desk awkwardly to pat her hand. "If I'm honest, we do the same thing with all other borrowers, only you just happened to not live in the county when it needed to be done. You will still need to file your claim, and we can help provide whatever documentation you need, but in the end you should see a sizable chunk of funds that should allow you to rebuild, even if it's not quite enough to bring the place into the luxury you originally had in mind."

"Well, that *is* good news," Henry said, still blinking in disbelief. "Getting the place insured was one of the first things on my list for when we got here. I don't know how we can ever thank you for that, sir."

Mr. Bullock waved it off. "Neighbors, McBride. It's what neighbors do. While we're talking about it, though, you'll probably want to talk to the sheriff about it before filing the claim. Last I heard he was investigating the cause of the fire, and the insurance company might want to know that."

"That's so helpful. Thank you. We're just—" Henry beamed at his wife in sheer relief. "We're just so pleased with everyone's reception since we got to Juniper Falls."

"I'm glad to hear it. Most of this town is good people. I'd hate for your first impression of the place to color everything else."

Charlotte could feel her entire body soften into the chair at the banker's news. However the tragedy had happened, it was done. What they needed now was, frankly, money and other resources to move forward. She was so overwhelmingly *relieved*.

"Now," Mr. Bullock said, "I know you did not plan to have to make this major investment, and I also know that it could be weeks before payment from the insurance company back East comes through, so I'm happy to offer you a short-term loan to help pay for construction in the meantime."

Charlotte and Henry exchanged another, startled glance. Though they would need to talk more about it— the idea of taking on more debt brought Charlotte's worry rushing back—the possibility of having all of this resolved so swiftly and smoothly was yet another relief.

"As far as getting the work completed," Mr. Bullock continued, "I've been giving it some thought, and I have a couple recommendations for you. As I'm sure you can imagine, most men around here have plenty of work for themselves, without extra time to take on building an entire hotel for someone else. That said, however, I do have a handful of names for you—"

"Mrs. Bennett gave us some names too," Charlotte interjected.

"Wonderful!" He beamed. "Maybe there's some overlap."

He flipped through a small collection of paperwork and pulled out a full sheet that he glanced at before pushing it across the desk to Henry.

"I'm happy to make any introductions you like, as well as vouch for the work ethic of any of these men. There's been a surprising amount of building in the acres around the town over the last few years. All of these men have plenty of experience."

"You have made all of this so easy for us," Charlotte said. "I can't thank you enough, truly. But also . . ." She paused, uncertain.

"What is it?" her husband asked softly.

Mr. Bullock leaned forward to hear her.

Charlotte's face heated, embarrassed. "I just can't help feeling like this is all . . . too good to be true? Yes, of course, the building burning down before we arrived is a tragedy, but ever since then everyone has been so kind, so helpful. I'm sure I don't understand how we can deserve such generosity."

"There's nothing to *deserve*," Mr. Bullock said, waving away her objections not unkindly. " 'Love thy neighbor as thyself' and all that. You're about to become one of the pillars of this town—or your business is, at least. I'm sure you will have more than ample opportunity to repay whatever assistance others are offering you now."

"I certainly hope so. I've already started thinking about some kind of party or gathering we could host for everyone."

"Let's not get ahead of ourselves," Henry said with mock panic. "The place doesn't even have a working front door yet."

"We'll get there, though. Especially with the help of such people as Mr. Bullock." She turned back to him. "Thank you again, so much. I cannot say it enough."

He smiled and stood, signaling to the McBrides that they were done.

"Have me over for dinner some night when your hotel chef is free," he said with a wink. "I'll be in Juniper Falls until they plant me toes-up, so there's plenty of time."

As Charlotte and Henry exited the bank, she gripped his arm and leaned in close. "He was so much kinder than I expected a bank manager to be," she said in a whisper.

"He's one of the reasons I thought this town might be good for us. His reputation with the bankers I know in Philadelphia is sterling."

The pair walked back out into the July afternoon, relieved that their biggest fear had been taken care of. On top of that, they seemed to have made one more friend, putting down another tiny root in their new home.

CHAPTER NINE

Nearly all of the residents of Edith's boarding house had left for the day. Mrs. Watkins sat quietly in the parlor, knitting something that was beginning to look like a sweater, but otherwise all the other men and women had gone off to their errands or occupations. This left Edith and Daisy to clean and cook and reset everything before the horde descended again in a few hours. Though she had never had children of her own, Edith imagined this must be at least somewhat what it was like to try to run a house with a big family. Trying to keep track of the cleaning and eating and other schedules of more than half a dozen people was a lot.

As she changed the sheets in the boys' room, Edith could not stop thinking about how Bill had acted that morning. He had often been tense, occasionally agitated, but always quiet about it. Something must have happened to bring out this streak in him.

She looked around the bedroom; Jack and Silas were generally diligent about keeping their space clean, but they were still young men just striking out on their own, only recently taking responsibility for themselves, and so still had the occasional blind spot. Edith would sometimes find a dirty mug or half-eaten apple sitting out, marring the wooden surface of their bureau. She did what she could for them, but did not envy whatever women they might one day marry.

Perhaps they would grow up a bit before then.

After changing the sheets on the bunkbed, she moved across the hall to do the same for the double bed the Watkinses slept in. They would be moving out within the week, as the new house they were building was almost finished.

Edith wondered idly if she could find another long-term boarder to take their room. Maybe Daisy had heard of someone looking. Or maybe the McBrides would want a second room for their daughter.

With the sheets changed, Edith carried an armful of soiled linens back downstairs. Tomorrow would be yet another laundry day, and given how hot the July weather was getting, she was not looking forward to so long spent over a fire heating the water they would need. Without prominent stains, the sheets would not need to soak overnight. Regardless, Edith knew there wasn't enough time left in the day for her to get it all done before dark that day.

Her projects seemed never-ending, almost as if they multiplied by themselves.

Thank goodness she had Daisy, she thought for what must have been the hundredth time.

Edith had just exited to the kitchen to start the

process of boiling water for her laundry when she heard a knock on the front door.

As she was sitting closest, Mrs. Watkins answered and soon was in the doorway to the kitchen informing Edith that Sheriff Sands had asked for her.

First Bill's nonsense and now this, she thought. It was a good thing she did not have too much planned that day that couldn't be moved.

She followed Mrs. Watkins back to the parlor, where the other woman collected her knitting and discretely went upstairs to leave Edith alone with her guest.

"Have a seat, Sheriff. Can I get you something? Is there anything I should be concerned about?"

"I don't need anything, thank you. I won't keep you long." He lowered himself gingerly onto the edge of the horsehair chair that sat across from the front window. As though to support his words, his body did not seem at all comfortable being there.

Edith sat on the sofa where Mrs. Watkins had been, but she, like the sheriff, couldn't relax either.

"The new folks—the family that bought the inn— they're staying here?"

"They are. News must travel fast. They've been in town less than a day, and you're now the second person to ask me about them."

"Really? Who else did?"

"Oh, one of the men that live here. He missed meeting them at supper last night." When she saw the sheriff's questioning expression, she added, "Bill Stuart."

"Hm. And these new people, did they say anything . . . interesting?"

"Interesting?" she repeated.

"Maybe something that raised questions or indicated that they might know more than they were letting on?"

"I don't think so. Really. I saw them standing outside the burned hotel not long after Bobby Cox brought them from the train, and they seemed . . . distraught, to put it mildly. I don't know how long it would have taken them to even find a place to stay if I hadn't introduced myself. He—McBride is their last name—Mr. McBride talked a bit about their train trip out from back East, and Mrs. McBride seemed to be consumed with making lists of what they needed to do now that the inn was not what they expected. But all that seemed . . . well, perfectly natural. In such circumstances, at least. I can't think of anything out of the ordinary, except for the fact that the inn had burned at all, and of course that was before they arrived."

"Hm," he said again, having nodded all through her description of the previous night.

"Is there something I should be looking for? Something I should be worried about, Sheriff? You would tell me, wouldn't you?"

"I will certainly tell you everything I can."

That was not a terribly reassuring answer, but Edith realized it was likely all she was going to get.

"To my knowledge," she offered, "Mr. and Mrs. McBride went to the bank first thing this morning to talk to Mr. Bullock about their financial considerations. It must have been quite the adjustment to their plans to discover the disaster once they got here. But I'm sorry, I don't really know anything more than that."

"I see . . ."

He finally settled deeper in his chair and leaned

back, thinking. Edith waited quietly. Sheriff Sands had only taken office a couple months previously, when the last sheriff had been revealed to be corrupt, helping some of the unscrupulous men in the town take over surrounding ranches. There had been deaths, and a hostage, and really more excitement than Edith was interested in. To this day she still wasn't quite sure who had even informed the US Marshal to come up from Cheyenne. Nevertheless, she was glad that mess was all over now.

In the aftermath of that adventure, Deputy Thomas Sands had been installed as the interim sheriff by the local federal marshal, subsequently winning the election held to make the position permanent. Though his authority and station were completely legitimate, and he had given no signs of the same corruption that had infected his predecessor, Sheriff Sands still seemed cautious. It was as though he was still becoming accustomed to it, still hesitant to be confident in what he did, still wary that he might be tarred with the same brush as had been Sheriff Vance.

She admired the man for his conscientious consideration of every detail that came across his desk, if nothing else, but his overserious nature made him seem even younger and more inexperienced than he was. She had an idea that once the man settled in more comfortably to his role and stopped second-guessing himself, he would enjoy himself much more.

But that brought her thoughts back around to what his role was in this investigation. It suddenly occurred to her that there could really only be one reason the sheriff was looking into something like a fire.

"Is it . . ." she began hesitatingly. "Sheriff, I have to ask. Is it possible the fire at the hotel was set on purpose? Should I be worried about my own home?"

"Mrs. Bennett." He smiled, a warm, reassuring expression that made her feel immensely more comfortable. "If I thought you were in danger, I would tell you. I promise. I take my role as protector and lawman very seriously. To tell you the truth, I am undecided on whether or not I think the fire was arson. That's what we're trying to figure out, and the more information I can gather the better."

"I'll let you know if I hear or see anything else. The McBrides don't know anyone in town other than Mr. Bullock, presumably, and now myself, but if anything changes . . ."

"I appreciate that. You never know what might spark something. Or who might let something slip." He paused, looking embarrassed. "That wasn't meant to be a joke about arson," he said seriously.

Edith could not help but laugh. "No offense taken, Sheriff. I understand."

He nodded. "Well, you tell me if you hear anything or think of anything more, will you?"

Sheriff Sands stood and offered Edith his hand.

She stood too. "I'll do that, Sheriff. I want everyone under my roof to feel safe and secure, so I will certainly try to be vigilant."

After he had thanked her and left, Edith sat on her sofa alone for another long moment. She had so much to do around the house, but her mind could not stop circling what the sheriff's visit had implied. She had lived in Juniper Falls for ten years now, and all her experience had been positive. There had of course been the unfortunate business the previous spring with the corrupt sheriff, and she had heard that the bank had been robbed not long before she arrived in town, but in general all of her neighbors were kind, all of them were generous, and all looked out for one another.

An accidental fire was a tragedy, but the idea that someone nearby could have burned down the hotel on purpose was frightening.

CHAPTER TEN

"Is there anything you need in town?" Lillian asked her sister while she tied on her bonnet. "From the general store or the butcher or . . . ?"

Mary Ann shook her head. She had just finished sweeping the front porch, and leaned the broom against the side of the house. "We have everything we need for supper, but thank you. I don't think we've checked for mail in a few days, though, and you know Ned was expecting a letter from his family."

"Oh, yes. Thank you for reminding me. Honestly, Mary Ann, if you were not here I feel like Ned and me would be living like unkempt orphan children."

She smiled. "Why are you going into town?"

"To be honest, I can't stop thinking about that new family and the hotel . . . The fire was bad enough, but you have to also assume that they don't have any friends here in town to lend a hand. I don't know what all I can do, but I won't stop thinking about it until I offer."

"All right. Well . . . have fun, I suppose. Not what I would choose," she said with a chuckle.

"You sure you don't need me to stay and help or bring you anything back?"

"Don't be silly. You deserve your time off before school starts again. And if you want to spend that time helping strangers, who am I to stop you?"

"You're the best," Lillian called as she finally exited to head into town.

Ned would not be happy that this was how she was choosing to spend her day, but that would be a problem for later. She needed to be true to herself, and right now that meant leaving the comfortable sameness of life at home and being of service.

This time of late morning there were not many people on the streets, and Lillian did not run into anyone she knew well enough to stop and chat. She debated with herself whether to try the hotel or the boarding house first, but even as she reached the main street of Juniper Falls she could see movement past the broken windows on the front of what had been the General Sherman Inn.

Someone was already there, presumably working.

She paused on the other side of the street, to watch without being seen. The daughter of the new family—a pretty girl no older than eighteen—was dragging a big piece of charred wood from the back to the front door. As Lillian watched, a foot-long chunk at the end broke off, unbalancing the girl in her labor. She stumbled briefly before squaring her shoulders and continuing without complaint.

This girl seemed like she could use some help.

Lillian approached cautiously, and the young woman did not hear her steps over the sound of her own exertion, displaying all the energy and vigor of a person who did not have a house or children to care for. Her light-brown hair had been braided and pinned up sometime earlier in the morning, but with all the activity there was a cloud of fine, loose hair sticking up in all directions. Lillian immediately resolved that she wouldn't mention it. Starting off a potential friendship with such a criticism would not help either of them.

The younger woman turned toward the door at that moment and stepped back in surprise, dropping the wood.

"Oh! Hello. I'm . . ." She looked around at her work. "Is there something I can do for you?"

"I was going to ask *you* that question," Lillian said with a laugh. "You're . . . I'm sorry I don't know your name, but your family are the new owners of the inn, aren't you?"

"I am!" The stranger wiped her hands on her apron and came to meet Lillian.

They exchanged names, greetings, short biographies, and though this young lady—Mattie was her name—stood speaking to her quite politely, Lillian could not shake the feeling that she wanted to get back to her work.

"If you don't mind my asking, what exactly are you doing here by yourself? Do you need help?"

Mattie looked around at the mess. "If you want to help, I won't stop you, but really I'm mostly just trying to sort through all this to make it easier for whatever men come in after me to rebuild. Make it worse before it gets better, and all that. It's not as though I have much else to spend my time on, since we just got to town and I don't know anyone. But I can identify garbage easily enough."

Lillian felt a surge of connection to this young woman. "Oh! My goodness, I know exactly what you mean. I am one of the schoolteachers here, but on summer breaks like this I tend to feel a little bit superfluous."

"Really?" Mattie's eyes widened in surprise. "But you're married, aren't you? How on earth do you get away with . . ."

Though she trailed off, Lillian laughed, knowing full well how she had intended to finish the sentence. Mattie bit her lip anxiously before Lillian responded.

"Get away with being *lazy*? Easy. My younger sister keeps house for us. Mary Ann. She's about your age and came West with us, and I honestly don't know what I would do without her. She's far more skilled and more organized than me. I feel quite spoiled most of the time."

"That sounds heavenly. My older sister invited me to stay with her and her family in Philadelphia, but I was afraid *I'd* feel superfluous."

"Exactly. You understand. Do you want . . . Have you eaten? Surely you can't keep doing this all day without a break?"

Mattie laughed. "To be honest, I hadn't thought that far ahead. Cross that bridge when I come to it, and all that. I had a big breakfast, but all this work is certain to make me hungry as soon as I stop to notice."

"Come home with me. You should meet Mary Ann,

anyway. We can all three of us eat together, and we can answer your questions about the town and you can regale us with tales of your fancy Philadelphia childhood."

Mattie laughed. "I fear you will be disappointed on that end, but a meal with new friends does sound delightful."

"Wonderful. I'm elated, really." Lillian laughed self-consciously. "Thank you. This is . . ."

She stopped herself. This young woman did not need to know the details of how despondent she had been lately. Mattie did not need to know that Lillian was clinging to her new friend like a life raft. It would be enough to have a new friend, and a new distraction over lunch.

"You'll love it," she concluded. "My sister is a wonderful cook."

In a few minutes, Mattie had apologized for her dirty hands, found her canteen, and then apologized again for the state of her appearance. Lillian did everything she could to make the newcomer comfortable. They walked the few blocks to the Fryes' home, and as soon as they stepped inside, Mattie was offered water, soap, and a mirror in the first bedroom down the hall so she could clean up. While she was busy doing that, Lillian quickly asked Mary Ann about setting a third place for lunch, and within only a few minutes all three women were sitting together over a meal of chicken salad sandwiches.

"Oh my goodness, this is amazing," Mattie said in delight. "I know eventually I will have to help cook, but as long as we're at Mrs. Bennett's I get to take advantage of everyone else's expertise."

"I'm happy to give you any tips," Mary Ann offered. "I've been doing this for Ned and Lillian for almost three years now, and I just love it."

"Tell me about Juniper Falls," Mattie said, taking a sip of lemonade. "Pa tells me it's mostly a ranching town, and I know it's a few miles off from the railroad, but otherwise anything would be new to me."

The sisters glanced at each other, and both excitedly began speaking at once. In the year they had lived there, Lillian had made a concerted effort to attend town festivals, patronize all the stores she reasonably could, and learn everything about everyone. She'd wanted to feel at home as quickly as possible, and she'd mostly succeeded. Mattie asked more questions, eating her lunch, until Lillian realized that she'd been talking so much she'd barely made a dent in her own meal.

"And, maybe you don't know the answer, but why was the inn named after General Sherman? That seems rather . . . incendiary, doesn't it? Even at this late date," Mattie prompted.

Lillian and her sister exchanged a glance.

"Well . . ." Mary Ann began, then paused.

Mattie looked from one sister to the other. "Tell me." Her eyes lit up with curiosity.

"There's nothing big," Lillian said. "Nothing that we know for certain. Only rumors and gossip."

"And we know what Pastor Langdon says about gossip," Mary Ann added.

Lillian nodded. "The man who owned the hotel before your folks, Mattie, was from Virginia, but his family fought for the Union in the war. His name was Carl Brown, and though try as I may, I've only heard bits and pieces of his story. From the little I've heard, it sounds like when South Carolina seceded he immediately packed up his wife and three children and moved just a bit north into Maryland. His sons joined the army, and they stayed out of the Confederate states as long as the war lasted. His two boys were killed in action, and his wife succumbed to pneumonia. And then, of course, when he and his daughter finally felt safe to go home to Virginia, their house had been looted, half of it burned, and neighbors had started encroaching on their farmland."

"Goodness, that's awful. To lose everything like that," Mattie said.

"Precisely," Lillian continued. "As best we can tell, it made him just . . . livid. More than anything, he wanted to punish his Confederate neighbors. I don't know exactly what happened in his hometown in Virginia, but his daughter eventually got married, and once she was cared for, it was very firmly suggested that he leave. Mr. Brown came West, ended up in Juniper Falls for whatever reason, and began the next chapter of his life running the hotel. I assume he named it after one of the most destructive Union generals simply to spite whatever Confederates that might have made their way to the Wyoming Territory."

"I definitely recall him pointedly asking newcomers who their family fought for," Mary Ann added darkly. "It was sad. He was so . . . *angry*."

Mattie's eyes got suddenly big. "You don't think he burned down the hotel after selling it to my parents, do you?"

"Not at all," Lillian said confidently. "No, he has a

very high sense of honor. He never would have done that. But that's not to say he didn't rile up someone else who might have."

"Or maybe it was just an accident," Mary Ann said pointedly. "So many men throwing their cigarettes and lit matches in every direction. Smoldering coals falling out of stoves. Candles or oil lamps falling over. It's a wonder *more* things don't burn down around here, especially with all these wooden frames instead of brick. It could have been anything."

"She's right," Lillian said, nodding, chastising herself for gossiping. "There are so many different reasons that building could have burnt. I'm just so sorry for your family that it happened when it did."

"Oh well." Mattie shrugged. "I suppose it could have been worse. My family could have been inside, or it could have been full of guests. Can you imagine if someone had gotten hurt?"

Lillian shuddered. "I'm glad that's all behind us, but I'm so sorry for what your family is going through."

Mattie smiled. "Thank you. But I feel like it can only get better. And now we'll have a blank slate to start from. The more I think about it, really, the more excited I am."

Lillian gestured to her new friend. "Now, you tell us about Philadelphia. If I talk any more, I'm *never* going to finish this sandwich."

CHAPTER ELEVEN

The McBrides had left the bank and their meeting with Mr. Bullock with far more hope and reassurance than they had entered with. There were resources, there was a plan, and there was a community of help that they could tap into. With the two lists of approved workers in hand, Charlotte and Henry spent much of the following couple days finding these men, interviewing them, getting all their questions answered, until they could finally make a decision. By the end of that week, the McBrides had put together their construction team.

Ralph Chandler would be their man in charge of the entire operation. He was well known in Juniper Falls for his attention to detail and his problem-solving when something inevitably went wrong on a big project like this. He had two grown sons who would also work on the project, and he would be in charge of hiring more labor as needed. Charlotte had already heard him mention a man in the next town over who specialized in plastering walls; he also planned on talking to the blacksmith about a new screen for the big fireplace in the lobby, as well as the best mason in Juniper Falls for brick repair.

While Charlotte had been consumed with helping her husband find the right person for this job, their daughter had kept herself occupied here and there. Though she'd felt bad about taking Matilda away from her sweetheart in Philadelphia, she could not be more grateful to have her here with them in Juniper Falls. The girl had plenty of energy and was unfailingly generous with her time. Charlotte was surprised the first time she returned to the inn and saw what Matilda had done. She was less surprised when she learned that the young woman had already made a couple friends.

Over the course of several days, all the small pieces of this enormous project fell into place. The crew had been hired, the insurance claim had been made, and, best of all, a trio of letters from the other McBride children arrived. Mr. Quinn made a special effort to bring them to the boarding house, and Henry tipped him handsomely for his effort.

After such a harrowing beginning, their move to Juniper Falls seemed to be finally settling into a comfortable routine. The rebuild would get them one step closer—and what a big step it was—to making a forever home in this frontier town.

The day Ralph was to start construction, Charlotte spent the first hour after breakfast trying to occupy herself and not let herself be distracted by thoughts of what was happening at the hotel. She had brought their ledger book, records of purchases, and bank statements down to the table in the dining room of the boarding house, and was trying to reconcile it all. After selling their home and most of their belongings back East, they had enough of a financial cushion that the expenses of their move thus far could be absorbed, but not so much that they could avoid paying attention to the budget any longer. She had hoped to go through all the transactions and expenditures from the last couple months now, so that they could be better equipped to make spending decisions during the construction period.

But she could not focus. It was as though the carefully written numerals swam in front of her eyes. She felt like she could hear every conversation going on everywhere else in the house, so scattered was her attention.

Finally, after sitting there long enough to be able to say that she had made a real effort, Charlotte gave up. She closed the ledger with a thump loud enough that Mrs. Watkins came to see what the ruckus was.

"Are you all right?" she asked with a frown, taking in the sight of all the notes and papers spread across the table in front of Charlotte.

"I'm all right. I just . . . I need to get out, I think. I can't sit still."

"Today is the day, huh?"

Charlotte nodded eagerly as she gathered up her loose piles and stacked them on top of the closed ledger. "Mattie did so much of the work to clean up the space that Mr. Chandler seemed very optimistic about making noticeable progress right away. And with everything we're spending, and everything we have invested in this new chapter, I need to just . . ." She picked up the rest of her things and started toward the staircase. "If I'm there, at least, I'll feel like I'm doing something."

"Balancing your books wasn't doing something?"

Charlotte laughed self-consciously. "Yes. It was. Or it would have been if I could focus on it." She turned and winked. "Don't tell my husband."

Mrs. Watkins smiled thinly at her. Over the week that the McBrides had been living at the boarding house, Charlotte had gotten the sense that the Watkinses, while perfectly nice people, did not share their sense of humor. They would be cordial without being intimate, and though that was perfectly fine with Charlotte, she hoped that she would soon have the opportunity to meet more female friends with whom she could laugh and dream and enjoy herself as they put down roots deeper and deeper in this new town.

Charlotte made a polite excuse and exited to take all her paperwork upstairs to her bedroom. After grabbing her bonnet—leaving a shawl, it was already too hot for the summer morning—she left again, stepping out onto the porch and looking out at Juniper Falls, this time on her own.

In the week since her family had arrived in Juniper Falls, Charlotte felt as though she had been busy morning, noon, and night. Now that Ralph and his team were taking over the project, however, she realized that she could take her time. She could pay better attention to the people and businesses of her new home. She could *breathe*. She did want to get to the hotel to see how the men were getting on with the project, but she could stroll instead of hustle to get there.

As she stepped off the path from the boarding house into the main street, a wagon passed her, pulled by two horses and piled high with crates full of fresh summer produce. Where the McBrides had lived in Philadelphia there had been similar wagons, riders, coaches, and other transportation rolling down the narrow stone streets, but far fewer than she saw here. There was just less of a need back East. The western frontier was so much more spread out than the dense urban centers of the eastern United States. In fact, Charlotte realized that they may need to buy horses themselves, an investment that they had never had to make before.

They would need to coordinate with Bobby Cox to make sure that someone could bring guests from the train to their hotel. They would need to plan any major purchase with far more forethought than they had back East, given how laborious it would be to have something shipped out here. They would need to allow for more time to get things done, with fewer people and fewer resources in this much smaller town.

As she walked, Charlotte realized she had gotten lost in her thoughts, planning for the future and guarding against any more catastrophe, and had not paid attention to the businesses or people all around her in that moment. She sighed, longing for the day when she could feel settled and content.

Today was not that day. There was just too much to do.

She noted the barbershop, laundry, and hardware store as she continued to walk down the street toward her inn. It was only a couple blocks from the boarding house, along Main Street. She crossed another wide street—Market Street—and spotted her inn on the next block. As she drew closer to what was left of the building, she was delighted to see four strong men moving in and out, hauling away trash and making way for pristine, fresh wooden boards. She'd had no idea where they would even be starting with construction, and seeing how much had been done already was exhilarating.

"Charlotte!"

Her husband had been the first to see her approach, and he came to meet her with a concerned expression.

"Is everything all right? Mattie all right?"

"Yes! Oh, darling, I didn't mean to worry you. I just could not think about anything but this building and the work, and so I decided to come see for myself."

"Smooth so far," Henry said, offering his arm to lead her back toward the building. "But then it's only been a few hours. Ralph estimated that we could get everything finished in about a month, but I'll have to ask him if he wants to amend that date now that we've gotten started and he's seen the extent."

"If he says a month, I will assume it will take two."

"My thought too," Henry agreed. "But I plan to be here every day to keep an eye on it. I don't know that I'm quite fit enough to help as much as the younger men, but I can do some of it."

"You're no longer a young man, my love," she said indulgently. "If only we had gotten one of our boys to come West too. They would have been so helpful already."

"Yes, but can you imagine fitting one of those tall boys in our already cramped room?" Henry laughed. "They'll be here soon enough, and I have no doubt that when that happens we'll have plenty of work for them."

"I tried to bring our ledger up to date this morning, but I didn't get very far. I'll try again this afternoon. I think now that I have seen with my own eyes that work has really started, and *something* has been done, I may be able to focus better."

"Well, you know, love . . ." He squeezed her in a sideways hug and kissed her temple as she continued to watch the laborers. "Just do what you can do. There's no rush. And remember that if all you get done is making a list of things to do and emptying your brain out, that's still something."

Charlotte laughed, a bit embarrassed. Her overactive mind was a regular joke between them, but it came with a heaping of truth. Planning made her feel more prepared, made her feel more capable, made her feel more worthy of the love of everyone around her. She did her best, but more often than not any sleep she lost was because she was awake thinking about what needed to be taken care of the following day.

"I'm not sure we have enough paper to capture all the thoughts that are constantly in my head."

Her husband laughed and hugged her again. "At least we know ours will be the best-prepared hotel west of the Mississippi River and everyone will know our name."

Charlotte sighed. She didn't say it out loud, but Henry's comment reminded her that she also needed to find the newspaper office and talk to the editor about how to place an advertisement here. And get information for how to place advertisements in other papers, and on and on and on . . .

There was a very good chance she would lose sleep again tonight.

CHAPTER TWELVE

Mattie had done everything she could do by herself—
with the occasional assistance from Mrs. Frye—in the
mess of the burned-out inn. It had taken several days,
but she had sorted through the charred wood, broken
glass, water-damaged furniture, and unidentifiable
detritus on the ground floor of the ruined hotel. There
was a chaotic pile near the open door of what she
assumed to be unsalvageable garbage, but there was also
a more organized stack, deeper in the lobby, of wood,
metal, and other pieces that Mattie suspected could be
reused somehow.

She was guessing, of course. This whole experience
was more involved than she had ever experienced,
though she supposed that was to be expected when
faced with such a tragedy for the first time. Every day
she felt like she was learning something new, or
embarking on some tiny adventure. Though of course
she would have preferred the hotel be standing when

they arrived in Juniper Falls, Mattie prided herself in always seeing the bright side of a situation.

On one of the final days there working by herself, Mattie was finishing cleaning up the lobby of the inn as best she could. One last sweep all the way around the room. She had finally made her way to the back corner underneath the staircase. To her untrained eye, it seemed like the damage was the worst in this spot, as though the fire had somehow been concentrated there. There were the barest remnants of a side table, broken into pieces and completely blackened as if used as firewood.

Mattie looked around and realized there were other spots in the lobby that had similarly intense fire damage, all along the baseboards, and at roughly regular intervals. She couldn't have noticed before, what with all the damaged pieces throughout the room. It was the strangest thing. She wondered how the fire could have jumped from spot to spot, before finally concluding that she must be imagining things. That was not how fires behaved, of course—not without a strong wind, at least —and anyway, if she was honest with herself, she did not know anything about it. Perhaps something big had broken, littering burning pieces throughout the room, or any number of explanations.

"I'm just looking for excitement," she said out loud to the empty room. "Focus, Mattie. That's nothing."

This was a thing she and Duncan had joked about over the years: about what a difficult time she had sitting still; about how quickly she could get bored of something. He had always been half-joking, half-serious in his worrying that she would hate to be a housewife, but

Mattie in turn had always insisted it was everything she wanted.

And now, here she was, inventing mysteries where she had no business doing so.

She picked up the charred remains of the table, but stopped when she noticed what was underneath. The floorboards had likewise been blackened by the fire, but somehow protected, wedged partially under the baseboard as though it had been kicked there, was a single, mother-of-pearl brown button.

She tossed the bits of the table into the pile with everything else that needed to be hauled away and quickly returned to pick up her find. It took her a second to dig it out from the spot where it had been wedged, and she was surprised to see how undamaged it was, but Mattie was excited. She held it in her palm, up to her face to take a closer look. The light layer of ash was easily rubbed off, and she realized upon looking closer that it still carried a single piece of thread, as though it had been abruptly pulled from a man's shirt.

There wasn't much she could do with a single button, but she had heard back in Philadelphia that some of the younger girls were making long charm strings to collect unique buttons such as this. Superstitions differed between if a girl collected a thousand buttons she would forever be a spinster, and if a girl collected a thousand buttons she would then meet her true love, but Mattie had a long way to go before that would be a problem.

She tucked the button away in the pocket of her apron and got back to work.

Mrs. Frye had not come by to help in a couple days, and Mattie let her mind wander to thoughts of what that family could be up to. She had been harboring small, secret hopes that Lillian and Mary Ann might be her first friends in this new place. Protecting that tiny ember of hope, reluctant to blow too hard on it, Mattie thought fondly of the lunch she had been invited to the week before.

Of course she knew she could not expect such hospitality all the time, and of course she knew that those two women had had entire lives before Mattie McBride came into town. But she longed for that connection again.

Maybe she would go to church the following Sunday. Her family had been too tired and frazzled the previous week to attend, but she bet she could talk her parents into it this week. Maybe then Mattie would have more friends here.

Maybe then she would be able to find some way to fill her time once the men took over the project of rebuilding the inn.

She'd left the broken mirror at the foot of the stairs for last, afraid of injuring herself and not being able to continue. But just as soon as she had bent down to grab the largest piece, she heard someone call her name.

"Miss McBride! Is there something I can help you with?" It was Mr. Chandler, and he hurried forward to take the large piece of broken glass from her. "You shouldn't be here by yourself."

She had been here by herself for several days already, but she knew better than to point that out to him. Instead, as she relinquished the mirror, she turned her attention to the other man, still standing in the doorway. The newcomer was about Mr. Chandler's own age, old enough to be her father, but she did not want to make any assumptions about his physical ability.

"Good afternoon," she said. "I'm Mattie McBride. My parents own this hotel. I don't think we've met yet. Will you be helping Mr. Chandler with the restoration?"

"Oh, no, not me."

"This is Mr. Lowry," Mr. Chandler said, holding the mirror pieces safely away from his body. "The building inspector from Cheyenne. He needs to go over the property so he can issue us a permit. We plan to start by the end of the week."

"Of course! I didn't realize that was today. I'll get out of your way."

She went to collect her canteen and bonnet, then remembered the button that she had found wedged under the baseboard. For a short moment she thought about telling Mr. Chandler and Mr. Lowry about it. Surely whatever this was, if it turned out to be important, should be brought to the attention of a man in charge.

But they had already moved on to the big glass window frames that lined the front of the building, measuring and discussing details, and had stopped paying her any attention. Maybe now was not the time for her to draw attention to anything that might delay the construction unnecessarily.

As she made her way toward the front door of the inn, Mr. Chandler smiled and waved to her without even pausing his conversation with the inspector, and soon Mattie found herself in the bright August afternoon on the main street of Juniper Falls with nothing to do.

There must be *something* she could do. Maybe she

would learn how to ride a horse, or plow a field, or . . . What else did folks do out here on the prairies, if they didn't have a home to take care of? There must be something. There were not the abundance of museums and parks and theaters of Philadelphia, but folks in the territories still needed to fill their time.

It was still early afternoon when she left the inn to look for something else to occupy her day. She thought about trying to find her way back to the Fryes' home, but she didn't want to be an obligation to these new women she had only just met. She thought about stepping into the seamstress's just to see what it might cost to have a new dress made, but she didn't have the money to spend and so would feel bad about wasting the woman's time. She even thought about ducking into the small library near the end of the street, but she had never been much of a reader.

Walking back to the boarding house, Mattie checked at the post office for a letter from Duncan, as she had on so many other afternoons. Indeed, she occasionally checked at other times of the day as well. She and Duncan had practically grown up together, and she wasn't sure they had ever gone more than a few days without speaking—not until she had boarded the train to the territories, that was.

There was—still—no letter waiting for her, but Mattie chatted with the postmaster, Mr. Quinn, for a few minutes. He was an older man, bald head gleaming with the light film of sweat. On previous visits, Mattie had learned he was a childless widower whose closest relative was a nephew who lived in New York. She couldn't imagine being alone like that, and so she tried to always take the time for a short conversation when she could. Today, when she'd complained about the heat of the August afternoon, he'd encouraged her to look forward to the autumn weather in just a few weeks.

"And then we'll have our annual harvest festival. Folks sometimes come from as far away as Cheyenne for that one. It's too bad your folks' hotel won't be done by then."

"Oh! I wonder if it could be," Mattie said excitedly. "Mr. Chandler is already there getting the building inspector to issue whatever permits and things. How long until the festival?"

Mr. Quinn chewed the inside of his cheek as he thought. "Third weekend in October. Two and a half months from now. You're right! It might get done at that. But I'm afraid getting the furniture in time is another matter."

Mattie groaned audibly. "You keep dashing all my hopes, Mr. Quinn."

The old man laughed at her teasing. "I'll tell you what I'll do. The store is expecting new editions of Montgomery Ward's catalog any day. When it comes in, I'll let you or your ma know. Maybe you can get in your orders just in time."

"That's so thoughtful. Thank you. But that reminds me, I should be getting back to the boarding house to tell my parents that the building inspection is happening. They're understandably anxious about getting everything done."

"You're a good daughter, Miss McBride," he said with a wink. "And I know I'll see you tomorrow in case that rogue Mr. Shaw of yours has finally sent a letter."

CHAPTER THIRTEEN

"Ask her!" Daisy insisted.

Edith opened her oven to check on the state of the bread she was baking. She had woken up late that morning, which meant that she had started the bread late, which meant that some of her guests had to eat their breakfast without toast. And while not a single one of them had complained, she still did not like feeling as though she was letting them down. Part of the room and board that they were paying for, after all, was a hot breakfast every morning.

"Ask her?" she said distractedly.

The bread was still several minutes away from being done. The bacon and potatoes had just finished frying, but she had not even started on the eggs that the Watkinses were ready for. She could feel them sitting at the dining room table, expecting her.

"Did you take the coffee in to Mr. and Mrs. Watkins?"

"Yes," Daisy said, still looking at her expectantly. "Are you listening to a word I'm saying?"

"I'm sorry, no," she admitted, straightening. "I'm all flummoxed today. I ran into the sheriff again yesterday, and he asked me more questions about the McBrides, and then I couldn't sleep because I was worried . . . It took me forever to fall asleep, so I got a late start, and now it feels like I'm going to be spending all day catching up. I'm sorry." She sighed. "Tell me again."

"I said that since you have plans to see Mrs. Langdon today, you should invite Mrs. McBride to go with you. Help her get to know the pastor's wife? Make a new friend? I'm sure she would appreciate it."

"Oh, goodness, I had totally forgotten about that. Maybe I should cancel and give myself a chance to get ahead on what we need for supper tonight."

"Absolutely not! You're going. You already planned your week around it, and anything else you are worried about, I can handle."

"But—"

"I promise," Daisy insisted, interrupting her attempt to deflect.

Edith cracked four eggs into the already hot cast iron pan. The yolks of three of them stayed intact, but the fourth broke, making the otherwise pristine meal just as messy as her day felt. But food was food, and she was always reminding herself that no one expected perfection from her.

"You know I'm right," Daisy prompted with a grin.

Edith pulled the bread out of the oven and set it on the counter next to the stovetop, with the empty plates waiting for the Watkinses' breakfasts.

"I think maybe I'll have you take these plates in, and then I can bring a platter full of toast for everyone in a few minutes."

"All right. I can take a hint. Just think about what I said."

"I will," Edith promised. "But no one is going anywhere before they have eaten breakfast, so this is what I need to be thinking about right now."

As she spoke, she dished the food out between the two plates while Daisy waited. She also needed to remember to start another pot of coffee brewing while the bread toasted, and Mrs. McBride and Mattie could be downstairs at any minute for their own breakfasts.

"I'm going to take these in," Daisy said, a plate in each hand, "and then you let me know what else you need me to do."

When Edith was left alone again, as she sliced the fresh bread—a smidgen too soon, but it could not be helped—she did think over Daisy's suggestion. Her plans with Mrs. Langdon that afternoon were intended to be tea with the pastor's wife, the schoolteacher, and several other women of the town to discuss the funds for the Juniper Falls school that they wished to raise before classes began again. If Mrs. McBride was interested in putting down roots in this town, this would be the perfect inroad for her.

Edith could hear the murmur of conversation in the dining room; though she could not make out any of the words, it did sound like two more women may have joined. Quickly, she put the bread in the oven to toast, added a few more slices of bacon to the frying pan to prepare for Mrs. McBride and Mattie, and moved to dicing another potato.

Daisy was right.

Daisy was usually right, and Edith had learned pretty quickly that her friend's knowledge and advice were a gift and that she would be better off listening to her in the first place, since she would more often than not end up listening to her anyway.

As she diced the potatoes and dropped the pieces into the pan next to the frying bacon, Edith thought back to her first few months after moving to Juniper Falls. She and her husband, Horace, had been so busy for the first couple months getting their home built, but once that had been done, before they had enough guests to keep her busy, Edith had been at loose ends, without friends, without children to fill her time. And then her husband had died, and she had been left alone in this small (then even smaller) town on the frontier, miles and miles away from everyone who loved her. She had gone to church by herself every week, slowly introducing herself to the other women of the town. Actually forging real friendships, however, had taken much longer.

If she could somehow guide Mrs. McBride through that difficult transition period, she would feel as though she had done some good.

Daisy returned to the kitchen and started the fresh coffee brewing without being asked. They worked in silence for only a moment before Edith spoke.

"I know you're right. I'll ask her to come with me."

She bent down to check on the toast, and Daisy was at her side in an instant.

"Should I box up some cookies or something for you all to take?"

"No. Mrs. Langdon assured us that nothing was needed."

"Mrs. Langdon is always a wonderful hostess. She'll be thrilled that you felt comfortable to expand the committee—but more than that, she'll be thrilled to be one of the first people who get to meet the newcomer."

Edith grinned at that. Mrs. Langdon was quite proud of her role in this small town as the pastor's wife. There were two churches in Juniper Falls, but Mrs. Langdon was determined that her husband's would be the preeminent one, and so took every opportunity she could to strengthen that position.

"I'm not going to tell you you're right again," she said, teasing.

Daisy laughed out loud.

"I'll take their breakfast in," Edith continued, "if you could start cleaning up in here for me."

Edith really did not even have to ask; Daisy was unfailingly thoughtful and aware of the various tasks that needed to be done, and as Edith dished up the hot meals for Mrs. McBride and Mattie, she began heating water in which to wash the soon-to-be used dishes.

With a plate in each hand, Edith entered the dining room and found the two McBride women sitting by themselves at the table, each with a half-full cup of coffee in hand. Across the table from them were the remnants of the Watkinses' breakfast, but the couple had evidently already left for the day.

That was somewhat of a relief to Edith—she did not think Mrs. Watkins would do well at the fundraising meeting, but neither could she think of an excuse not to invite her.

"What do you ladies have planned today?" she asked as she served the breakfasts.

"We were just discussing that when you came in. Matilda has her regular pilgrimage to the post office, and we thought we might check in on the men's progress, but until we have a better idea of when the inn will be finished or we can order the furniture we need, there's not much point in doing much else."

"Well, if you are free . . ." Edith sat at the table across from them, collecting the dirty dishes into a stack in front of her. "I have joined the committee to raise money for the schoolhouse for the upcoming year. We have a meeting this afternoon at the pastor's house to start to plan our big fundraising event. If you'd like to come with me, I'm sure Mrs. Langdon would be thrilled. And you can also meet some of the other ladies of Juniper Falls who take an interest in helping."

"Ooh! I want to go," Mattie said immediately, turning to her mother. "I'm going. Please, oh, please let me go. I need more people in my life, and I haven't the slightest idea how to go about that." She turned back to Edith and added, "No offense meant, of course."

Edith chuckled as she stood again. "None taken, and you are more than welcome. We need to leave here about twenty till two, to walk the couple blocks to the end of Main Street." She turned toward the mother. "Mrs. McBride? Does that sound like something you would like?"

"Fundraising?" She looked wary. "What will be expected of us?"

"Nothing more than you are willing to offer. It's not that kind of committee, but especially not during your first meeting. If, as we talk over the event and what is needed, you find yourself wanting to volunteer for a task or responsibility, you can do that. Otherwise, if you want to just join me to listen and meet the other women, I promise that will be perfectly all right too."

Mrs. McBride considered this for a long moment before nodding, seemingly resolute. "Yes. Thank you. That sounds like exactly what I need."

"What *we* need," Mattie added.

Accordingly, a few hours later, the two women met Edith on the front porch and began their walk to the other side of town. The Langdons lived in a small parsonage on the same property as Everlasting Grace Church, where Main Street met Church Street before continuing on to the edge of town. A row of juniper trees lined the edge of the church property, creating a kind of hedge between the place of worship and the pastor's house. The three women walked up the narrow path between them, following another pair of women who had arrived just before them but who were let in right away.

They reached the porch, and the front door swung open before Edith had even finished knocking.

"Good afternoon, Mrs. Langdon. I hope it's all right that I brought Mrs. McBride with me," she said immediately. "And this is her daughter, Matilda. They are both very keen to be involved."

The surprise on Mrs. Langdon's face was evident, but she quickly covered this up and greeted her new guests.

"Of course! Welcome, Mrs. McBride. Miss McBride.

I heard you all had arrived to take over the inn. I've been hoping for a chance to meet you. Please come in."

In moments, the two new women had been ushered into the parlor where most of the other ladies had already taken seats. Edith hung back, watching a bit anxiously, but with the satisfaction that she had done a good deed. Mrs. McBride seemed even more pleased to be part of the committee now that they had arrived than she did when she was invited, and Mattie had the look of a child who had walked into a candy store. Even if this meeting might be taking time out of her day that Edith did not feel she could spend, she had to admit she was doing good work for this family.

CHAPTER FOURTEEN

Lillian sat on the stiff, wooden dining chair that had been brought into the Langdons' parlor for extra seats. She was one of the youngest of the committee, and would stand to benefit the most from what they were doing; she could certainly suffer through a slightly uncomfortable chair for the next hour. With her hands clasped in her lap, she watched the other women around her, waiting for the pastor's wife to take charge of the meeting.

She had been interested when Mrs. McBride entered, but perked up even more when she noticed Mattie right behind her. Lillian had been wondering what the other woman would do to fill her time, now that Mr. Chandler and his team had taken over the rebuilding of the inn. Seeing Mrs. Langdon bring in more chairs from the dining room, Lillian scooted her own over to make room for her new friend to sit by her.

"It's so good to see you again," Mattie whispered excitedly as she took her seat in the wooden chair next to her. "I was afraid I'd go crazy waiting for the inn to be finished, but then Mrs. Bennett told us about this meeting."

"I should have invited you myself," Lillian admitted, suddenly mortified. "I don't know what I was thinking. I'm so sorry."

But Mattie waved off her protests. "I'm here now. And you'll never be rid of me."

There were a few minutes of shuffling, introductions, another knock on the door, and everyone getting settled before the clock on the mantle ticked over to two o'clock. Of the fifteen women crowded into the pastor's parlor, Mattie caught the names of about half of them. But she focused, determined to learn the rest as the meeting continued and not give Mrs. Bennett any reason to regret inviting them.

"Welcome, ladies," the pastor's wife said, calling for their attention. "Let's bring this meeting to order. Mrs. Griffin sent a note to let me know her littlest is sick"— this was greeted by little sounds of sympathy around the room—"which means I think everyone we were expecting has arrived. Thank you so much for coming to my home. Please help yourself to the coffee and cookies." She gestured to the small table in the middle of the room. "Anna was quite excited to be able to bake for you all yesterday."

Lillian smiled. Anna Langdon was one of her students. Only a child and already baking a few batches of cookies. If only she applied that kind of diligence to her spelling; despite being the pastor's daughter, she regularly mixed up *angle* and *angel*.

"Is Anna her daughter?" Mattie whispered.

"Eight years old," Lillian whispered back, nodding.

With raised eyebrows, Mattie leaned forward and helped herself to the first of the thumbprint cookies.

"As you know, our goal for this year's fundraising event is to be able to pay for a new coat of whitewashing and a row of juniper trees for the schoolhouse grounds. If we are so blessed as to raise more money, we will tuck it away to help defray the cost of any damage suffered to the school building over the winter. The terrible snowstorms of two years ago necessitated the school being closed for several additional weeks just to patch up the roof, and I personally vowed that we would never again find ourselves limited by resources should such a situation occur again."

Mrs. Trill raised her hand briefly before asking, "We have not decided what that event will be, though, have we? The fundraiser?"

Mattie leaned forward to snag two more cookies, handing one of them to Lillian.

"We had discussed some options a few months ago," Mrs. Langdon was saying, "but no, nothing has been decided. I thought we could spend today's meeting discussing and making that decision, so we can better divide up the responsibilities to pull the whole thing off."

Mrs. Langdon looked around the room as she spoke; in Lillian's experience, few people were willing to contradict her, or even interested in doing so. The pastor's wife both had the gift of leadership as well as the gift of charm. More often than not, whatever conclusions she came to were the best of whatever options were available, as she had already done all the preparation, research, and considerations necessary and merely presented what she had already settled on. And she never seemed to have any trouble getting everyone else to agree with her.

"I think," she continued, "that given previous successes as well as the amount of money we are looking to raise, and considering the talent and resources we have available, the most likely option will be to host a Christmas concert of some kind, letting the students perform. We can make money on both ticket sales as well as refreshments. That means, of course, that we will need committees for the location and decorations, for the rehearsals and music, for food and drink . . . Is there anything I'm forgetting?"

Mrs. Langdon looked at all the women in her living room expectantly, though in Lillian's estimation it seemed as though the pastor's wife had once again thought of everything. Opening the floor to more suggestions seemed like merely a polite gesture.

Mattie raised her hand, beginning to speak before the pastor's wife had acknowledged her. "We probably need a committee for promotion, too, don't we? To make sure that as many people know about the event as possible?"

Mrs. Langdon pursed her lips, thinking. "Well, the parents of the performers will know, certainly. And my husband can announce it from the pulpit. But, yes, maybe a small committee to further encourage people to come could be useful."

"I'm sorry," Mrs. McBride spoke up. "My daughter and I are new to Juniper Falls. Maybe I just am not clear on how all this works. Is the Christmas concert something that was already decided before today, or are there other options we need to discuss or vote on or . . . ?" She looked around the room uncomfortably, her question trailing off. "I'm sorry, I'm just trying to understand."

"No need to apologize," Mrs. Langdon said, smiling. "You are absolutely right to have questions. I'm afraid I'm getting ahead of myself. Who else has a suggestion for what kind of fundraising event we could do for the benefit of the school?"

Lillian looked around the room. There were something like fifteen women of various ages and family commitments present. Some she knew well, as mothers of her students; some she knew only a little, like Mrs. Chandler. But one thing that all of the women had in common, Lillian suspected, was that every single one of them—except, of course, the McBride women—had come to this meeting assuming that Mrs. Langdon would have the best idea to accomplish what they needed.

After almost a full minute of silence, none of the other women speaking up, Mrs. Langdon smiled. "Well, this is flattering. If no one has another idea, shall we move forward with the Christmas concert?"

There were nods and murmurs of assent throughout the room. Lillian noticed that Mrs. McBride was blushing furiously, and looking at her hands clasped in her lap, perhaps in an attempt to hide said blushing. Lillian felt a bit bad for her; the newcomer was trying so hard to be useful, to fit in.

"Well, then, if there are no other concerns or questions, ladies, why don't we divide up into the various committees outlined? Let's see who wants to volunteer for which job first, and then maybe we can reassign as needed."

Lillian got lost in the general hubbub as women stood to move about the room, talk to friends, confer on decisions, and form into smaller groups.

"Which committee do *you* want to be on?" Mattie asked her. "Since the promotion was my idea, I suppose I should volunteer for that."

"You don't have to. If there's something you would rather do, you should speak up."

"No, I don't mind. I think perhaps I don't want to be on the same committee as my mother." She grinned. "But otherwise, I'm happy to help wherever I'm needed. Wherever you think you'll go, I could follow."

Lillian looked around the room again, where clusters of women were already forming in three corners. She knew from previous events that Mrs. Trill would be the first person on the food and drink committee, and that Mrs. Langdon would assess which committee was the weakest and assign herself there. There was Mrs. McBride, standing between two of the groups of women, looking a bit overwhelmed and lost. There was Mrs. Bennett, coming to Mrs. McBride's side to whisper some comfort or instruction. From where Lillian and Mattie sat along the edge of the room, she could watch all of this.

"Oh, good," Mattie murmured, also seeing her mother. "I think Mrs. Bennett will be good for Mama. Help keep her on an even keel until she gets used to this place."

"Is your mother easily excited?"

"No, it's more that . . . she just wants so badly to be

loved and useful that she goes way overboard with . . . with everything, really. She means well, but she tends to lose herself in the trying to help sometimes. I've seen her act as though she loved black tea for months because she thought that's what would make the other person like her more."

"I'm sorry to say it," Lillian said with a laugh, "but I think Mrs. Langdon will love that about her."

Mattie laughed, too, then shrugged. "Oh, well. As long as she's not volunteering *me* for anything, I don't mind." She stood and looked around. "I do think I will join the promotional committee. Which of these groups do you think that would be?"

Lillian stood next to her friend and looked at the three clusters of women and, balanced against what she knew of all of them, said, "I think maybe it's you and me. Mrs. Trill"—she pointed—"will be food and drink. Mrs. Thrush and Miss Wright are usually interested in decorations, so they'll be on the venue committee. And then Mrs. Armstrong has always played piano for concerts like this, so she'll be on the rehearsals committee. So that just leaves us."

"Mrs. Langdon did say it would be a small committee. But don't feel like you need to stay here with me. You should go . . ." Mattie gestured to the room at large. "I promise I'll be all right on my own."

"Girls, do you know what you're doing?" Mrs. Langdon had left her cluster to come speak to Lillian and Mattie. "I can ask another to come join you if you think you need more help getting the word out about our little concert."

Mattie and Lillian exchanged a look. Mattie shrugged, and Lillian turned back to the pastor's wife.

"I think we'll be all right, Mrs. Langdon. But we'll be sure to ask again if this turns out to be too much for just us."

She smiled at them and moved to the next group of women.

Mattie leaned toward Lillian excitedly. "So, when is the first meeting of our subcommittee?"

CHAPTER FIFTEEN

Charlotte positioned her hat, secured it with two pins, and then examined herself in the boarding house mirror for a full minute. Her graying, light brown hair fell in soft wisps around her face; her crow's-feet were hard to spot in this low light. Her dress was the same worn, traveling dress she'd had on through most of their train journey west, but at least it was clean.

Maybe one day in the future, when they were settled, when the inn was finished, she would have the money and time for a new dress. There was a seamstress in this town, she'd seen the store near the inn, and soon she could treat herself for the first time in a while. But not just yet. So much work to be done before then. She sighed and tried to smooth down the fraying edge of her lace collar.

"Mama, come on," Matilda said. She had appeared at her mother's shoulder and was also looking at her in the mirror. "You look fine. We need to go."

"Fine?" She turned to her daughter. "Just fine?"

"You look lovely, and you know as soon as we go downstairs Pa will say the same. Come on." Matilda tugged her mother's arm gently.

Over breakfast that morning, Mrs. Bennett had offered to walk to church with the McBrides—not because they needed the guidance, but just to help them feel more at home and to facilitate any introductions necessary when they got there. Charlotte was nervous. She knew she could expect kindness from her neighbors, but still felt the pressure of being what they needed her to be. The meeting of the fundraising committee Mrs. Bennett had taken Charlotte and Matilda to a few days prior had been just as welcoming as she'd hoped, but attending church was a far bigger matter. Far more people, far more expectations. Charlotte could not help but be immensely aware of what folks of the town might want of her and her husband as they endeavored to run a reputable, pillar business here in Juniper Falls.

Mrs. Bennett and Henry were both standing in the parlor waiting when Charlotte came down the stairs, Matilda close behind.

"Ready?" their landlady asked brightly. "You'll love it! I have no doubt."

They were running a little late, however, and by the time they had arrived at church the bell was already being rung and the congregation was finding their seats. Mrs. Bennett did not have a chance to do so much as wave to a couple friends before Pastor Langdon began his opening prayer. She led them to seats near the back of the church for the duration of the service.

Afterward, however, Mrs. Bennett leaned over and whispered, "I'd love for you to meet Sheriff Sands. He's not always here, but I spotted him up front. And you should probably also meet Mr. or Mrs. Eaton. They'll be your best source for produce for your inn. The Sunshine Cafe uses them."

Charlotte nodded, trying to remember all the names her friend had said. She was already overwhelmed. Matilda had already darted off to the other side of the room, where she evidently had spotted a friend. Henry had done the same, albeit more slowly. Charlotte and Mrs. Bennett had only just stood when they were stopped from leaving their row by Mrs. Langdon, who was approaching from the center aisle.

"Mrs. McBride, I'm so pleased you could make it." The pastor's wife beamed at her, making Charlotte feel as though she were the only person in the room. "What did you think of the service?"

Charlotte glanced at her husband, already deep in conversation with another man, who was nodding vigorously at whatever Henry was saying.

"It was lovely. The pastor seems so . . . compassionate."

"He is. We're really proud of the community we have built here over the last dozen years. But that also means that anyone and everyone here should be someone you need to know. Who can I introduce you to?"

"Oh!" Charlotte felt flustered, put on the spot like this. "I'm not sure . . . In the last week or so since we arrived, we have met so many kind folks. Mr. Bullock at the bank, and Mrs. Bennett, and Ralph Chandler and his boys . . . all the women at the fundraising committee the other day . . ."

Mrs. Langdon fixed her with an appraising eye.

"What about the sheriff or deputy? Not that there is all that much crime here in Juniper Falls, but it would never hurt to make sure that the lawmen know you, your husband, and your business, right?"

"Well, I pray there's no reason we need to seek them out later."

"Precisely. So let's go make friends now!"

Mrs. Langdon looped one arm through Charlotte's and looked around at the crowd of townsfolk pouring out of the wide front door of Everlasting Grace Church and milling about the grass lawn.

"Ah. There he is." She pointed to a broad-shouldered man on the fringe. "Sheriff Thomas Sands. Just took the position a few months ago. Come on."

With a gentle tug, Mrs. Langdon was leading Charlotte through the crowd, smiling, apologizing, squeezing between people, until they were standing just next to the sheriff. He glanced at them as he wrapped up his conversation with Mr. Thrush, of the General Store, before turning his attention fully to the pastor's wife.

"Mrs. Langdon. A pleasure." He looked at Charlotte, but waited to be introduced.

"Sheriff, I'm so glad I caught you," the pastor's wife was saying. "You know, I'm sure, that the General Sherman Inn has new owners. This is Mrs. McBride. She and her husband and youngest daughter have come all the way out from Philadelphia to take charge of it, and I told her that you were one of the men worth knowing in this town. Let me introduce you."

"Mrs. McBride," he said, offering his hand. "I've been meaning to look you up. I'm so sorry about the tragedy.

I do hope that you've found the assistance you need to rebuild."

"Oh, thank you so much," she gushed, flattered that this important man was paying attention to her family. "I admit it has been . . . trying. Certainly far from what we expected when we got on the train to come here."

"We still don't know how that fire happened, do we?" Mrs. Langdon asked.

The sheriff shook his head. "We're looking into it. I'm afraid I don't have any more news than that, but rest assured that if Deputy Inglis and I discover anything of note, we will be sure to let you know."

"We're staying at Mrs. Bennett's boarding house until the inn is rebuilt. Mr. Chandler estimated three or four weeks, but I'm telling myself I'll be happy if we're able to move in before the first snowfall."

He chuckled. "Chandler is a good man. He'll tell you the truth, but it is always best to take the unexpected into consideration."

"That's the only way I got through thirty years of raising half a dozen children," Mrs. McBride said. "Do you have children, Sheriff?"

"No, ma'am. No wife either. I hesitate to inflict this life—outlaws and firearms—on a woman. Haven't met the right one yet."

"I'm still keeping an eye out for you," Mrs. Langdon said.

"Thank you, ma'am." He smiled and tipped his hat to them. "If you ladies will excuse me, I need to have a word with Mr. Cox before he is off to Laramie again."

As the sheriff walked away, the two women turned back toward where the crowd was thinning out after the church service. Many of the families had started their way back home again for a big supper and a day of rest, though there were still some stragglers standing around talking.

Charlotte noticed Matilda chatting away with the schoolteacher and smiled in satisfaction. Though she knew it was likely that Duncan Shaw would send for her daughter to come back to Philadelphia to be married, she could not help hoping that Matilda would find her place here in Juniper Falls and stay. Only having one of her five children with her was difficult, and Charlotte wasn't sure she could stand to lose the last one.

"Oh, I had hoped to introduce you to Miss Flynn, our seamstress. I'm sure you're just dying for a new dress or two. But it looks like she's gone already. Next week, maybe?"

Mrs. Langdon looped her arm through Charlotte's again and walked them both slowly back toward the double front doors of the church building. Charlotte could not help but feel self-conscious about her dress, after that comment, but she tried to put it out of her mind.

"I can't thank you enough for how welcoming you have been," she said. "The committee. Church today. I promise as soon as we have our own roof over our heads I would love to have your family over for supper at least once."

"We would love that. But remember that there is no expectation whatsoever. Love thy neighbor as thyself, you know. We're happy to do what we can, knowing that if the situation was reversed you would as well."

"I have to say . . ." They had stopped at the foot of

the stairs that led up to the church entrance. The pastor was closing the doors and locking them. As Charlotte continued, he came down to meet his wife and listen. "I know we've only been here a little over a week, but this town is so much different from our home in Philadelphia. I grew up in that city and didn't know any different. We had our friends, and our church, the children's school, but everyone there was so concerned with their own lives, protecting the small space that they had carved out for themselves, that it seemed like they didn't have the time or resources to be generous. Here, though . . ."

She looked around again at the few families still milling around, noticing how friendly and warm everyone seemed to be. All the families that had lived here for years and years had really made Juniper Falls a home.

"I'm looking forward to settling in here, and to being able to put down roots like you fine folks have done."

"Well, we welcome you to Juniper Falls," the pastor said, taking his wife's hand in his own. "Your inn will be the perfect way for you and your family to establish your presence in the community, and we're happy to help in any way we can."

CHAPTER SIXTEEN

When Mattie followed her parents back to the boarding house that Sunday afternoon after church, she felt as if she were floating. Being among all those people—their new neighbors, possibly new friends—had been precisely what she had been missing in the weeks since they had left Philadelphia. She felt more grateful than ever that she had never had trouble making friends, and wished that she could simply jump ahead to several months from now when she had met everyone and formed connections and shared jokes.

Lillian Frye was sweet, and though she was often quiet and kept to herself, as one of the teachers in Juniper Falls she seemed to know everyone and to be well liked. Over the few minutes that Mattie had talked to her after church, no fewer than four different people had stopped, interrupted, and told Mrs. Frye how much their child was looking forward to school in the fall.

Which meant that Mattie got to meet those people too.

She wished that she'd had a chance to join one of the larger committees for the fundraising event, but she consoled herself with the realization that being in charge of promotion all but guaranteed she would have a reason to talk to more people.

She practically skipped all the way home, so satisfied was she that, however long she lived in Juniper Falls, it would be an interesting adventure.

In spite of all that, she missed Duncan. He had been her best friend for years, and then her betrothed, and until her parents told her about the inn here, she had never thought they would be apart. It would have been so fun to talk to him about the changes they were making to the inn and the ideas she'd had to promote the school concert. Though she still had not received a letter from him, Mattie had been working on one herself for the last week. She decided that would be how she spent the rest of her day—finishing writing his letter.

Accordingly, the following morning after breakfast, Mattie left the boarding house for the general store. Mr. Quinn told her not to expect it to get back to Philadelphia for weeks.

"But we should be getting more mail delivered here in the meantime. Maybe your beau will have sent something too."

After the general store, Mattie had some time before when she and Lillian had agreed to meet to discuss their plans. There was still so much of Juniper Falls that she hadn't seen, people she hadn't met, things she hadn't experienced. As she exited onto Main Street, Mattie turned left and strolled slowly down to the cafe, stopping to look into every storefront as she did.

The newness of this place was far more exciting than she had anticipated. Mattie had expected to be bored on the frontier, in this small town without the commerce and conveniences of her home back East. But in fact the opposite was true. Because the people of Juniper Falls did not have the same access to things like factories or even ships to bring them whatever they could dream of, there was far more innovation, making one thing work in place of another that was otherwise unavailable. Because there were not big construction companies, she could easily find herself helping Ralph Chandler with the rebuilding of the inn. Because there were not the same social class expectations, Mattie had the chance to befriend anyone she chose.

Already she could tell that, whenever Duncan did send for her to return to Philadelphia to be married, she would miss this lively, earnest frontier town.

She crossed the street and reached the Sunshine Cafe about ten minutes before Lillian was supposed to meet her. When she entered, Mattie was delighted at the warm welcome. She stood in the doorway for a moment, looking around.

Jack Kinsey waved to her from across the room, and as she waved back, a bustling older woman came to the door to meet her.

"Morning, sunshine," she said, pulling a pencil from behind one ear. "You here to meet someone?"

"My friend should be here soon. Could we have a table for two, please?"

The woman guided her to a small table by the front window, where Mattie could watch the street.

"Should I bring you coffee while you wait?" she asked, as Mattie took her seat.

"I would love that."

The woman nodded briskly and set off back toward the kitchen. Mattie took a deep, satisfied breath, leaning her head on her hands and watching the Main Street of Juniper Falls.

The waitress brought her coffee and left her alone again to wait for Lillian, though Mattie could have sat there alone for a long time. Sitting so close to the window almost helped her imagine that she was in the middle of Main Street just a few feet away. The cafe sat directly next to her family's inn. From where she sat she could see none of the construction going on, but the stagecoaches, boys running and other pedestrians passing by and men heading into the saloon across the way caught her eye. When Lillian finally slipped into the chair across from her, Mattie had been so engrossed in the scene outside that she was a little startled.

"I'm sorry I'm late," Lillian said breathlessly.

"Are you? I didn't even notice. Don't worry at all."

"Morning, sunshine," the waitress said, appearing at their table with all her attention on Lillian.

"Good morning, Mrs. Jenkins." Lillian smiled. "Do you have any cobbler today?"

"We do! I haven't told your friend the specials yet, since she was waiting for you."

"Oh," Lillian said. "This is Miss Mattie McBride. She and her parents are new to town. They're taking over the General Sherman Inn. Mattie, this is Mrs. Jenkins. She and her husband have run this cafe for . . . what? Five years?"

"Seven," she corrected. "And, oh, honey, we were all so sorry to hear about the fire. I trust your parents have found the help that they need? We've been noticing all the work starting in the last few days."

"Thank you, yes, I think so. My mother doesn't love that I tend to jump in to whatever needs doing, so she tends to not tell me when there's a problem."

"Ah, well, mothers will do that." Mrs. Jenkins turned to Lillian. "Did you want a cobbler, honey? Fresh berries today. And a coffee?"

"I would love that."

"I'll have the same," Mattie said.

When Mrs. Jenkins left again, Mattie sat up proudly, gesturing to the room at large.

"Well. Shall we begin? Welcome to the first meeting of our promotion committee for the Christmas concert," she said grandly.

Lillian laughed. "I didn't realize you were going to take this so seriously."

"Of course I am!" she replied, in mock outrage. "Raising the funds for the education of the young people of Juniper Falls is very important. Even I don't have any children myself there."

"Very noble of you."

Mattie grinned. "At your service."

"I'm sorry," Lillian said, being serious again as Mrs. Jenkins silently served her coffee. "I didn't really have a chance to think about what we needed to do. My husband is redoing a whole display in his store and needed my help with that over the last few days."

"Oh, but I did. Mrs. Langdon offered to have it announced from the pulpit, so maybe we just need to make sure to remind her of that a few times between now and Christmas. And then when school starts, maybe we can make some handbills to send home with the students?"

"Maybe we should start that now. There are a lot of students. It's going to take us some time to write all that out."

"We can start once we know the details—date and location and things. But couldn't we have them printed somewhere? Surely we don't have to write all that out by hand."

Lillian frowned. "I didn't even think of that . . . But you're right."

"I guess I'm just used to living in a city big enough where *everything* is an option. You should have seen the hubbub when Mr. Werner on the next block got an ice box." She laughed. "What about the newspaper? Surely they want . . . news, don't they? And maybe they'll let us use their printing press to make the handbills."

"The *Gazette*?"

"Is that what it's called?" Mattie laughed. "Yes. That. Who do you know at the *Gazette*?"

"No one well. Mr. Sharp, the editor, is the only person who works there full-time, but there are two or three part-time people too. I'll ask my husband if he knows any of them. Since his shop is right on Main Street, I imagine he runs into other merchants often."

"Perfect. So, we have a plan then. And I'll keep thinking. This is the kind of idea-generating I love. But I have to warn you—if I suggest something that seems too far-fetched or unacceptable for this town, you have to let me know. Sometimes I don't realize when I've gone too far down a particular path."

"Here you are, ladies," Mrs. Jenkins said as she set down plates in front of each of them. "Fresh berry cobbler. We're bound to run out by midafternoon, so I'm glad you came in early."

"Mrs. Jenkins," Mattie said, catching the older woman by the hand before she walked away again. "If we made handbills to promote the school fundraising event in a few months, do you think we could leave some in here for your patrons? Maybe a stack by the front door or . . . I don't know. We could plaster one in the front window?"

"Hm. I'd have to ask my husband about that. Not that we object to the school, you understand, but rather to the clutter. I'm not sure we want to bombard our guests with that kind of thing."

"See?" Lillian said in a quiet voice after the older woman had left. "This isn't going to be easy. Fundraising alone is asking for things, but at least that way people see the clear way their money will be benefiting someone else. This kind of begging is a far different thing."

"Well . . ." Mattie picked up her fork. "We'll just have to figure out a way to word it so that it doesn't feel like begging."

The two women ate and chatted for nearly another hour, Mattie peppering Lillian with questions about the town and the people, really pressing her to search her mind for ideas of who might most readily agree to help.

"What would be easiest," Lillian said mischievously, "is if we could just talk Mr. Harmon into donating all the money we need, and then we could skip the concert altogether."

"Mr. Harmon is the . . . rancher? I'm usually good with names, but I've had to learn so many lately."

Lillian nodded. "Richest man in the county. I don't know that he would even miss the two hundred dollars that Mrs. Langdon set as the goal. Which reminds me—it's almost time for the next meeting at her house. We should go."

"What will she think of our idea?" Mattie asked, as they each pulled out money to pay for their meals.

"I'm not sure. Maybe we wait to tell her until we actually have something specific to report?"

"I love that idea. A grand reveal."

"We just need to figure out what we're going to reveal," Lillian said, as the two women giggled.

CHAPTER SEVENTEEN

Mattie left to meet a friend and Edith heard the front door close behind her. She cleared the dishes from the breakfast table, eager to get started on the rest of her chores for the day. Captain Stuart had not yet made an appearance that morning, but it was possible that he hadn't slept there at all the night before; she wasn't sure whether or not to expect him for breakfast, and she wasn't about to wait around for him.

As grateful as she was to have a nearly full boarding house, Edith had to admit to herself that she would be just as grateful when the captain moved on—though she had no inkling of when or why that may occur. In the meantime, she would simply do her best to not set off one of his angry tirades or impulsive spirals. He seemed to be a man who needed something. Help of some kind. The best she could do, she told herself, was feed him and keep a roof over his head.

She carried the dirty dishes into the kitchen, where

Daisy had already started washing the pans used to make the meal.

"Today is the day Mr. and Mrs. Watkins move into their new house, isn't it?" Daisy asked as she dried the frying pan. Edith set the last of the dirty dishes on the butcher-block counter next to her. "Do you think they'll need any help with that?"

"I know Mr. Watkins asked Silas if he could help load up their wagon before he headed out to the ranch, but I don't know what they might need beyond that." Edith leaned against the counter and crossed her arms over her chest. "They ate breakfast very quickly and hardly said a word to me. There must still be some packing to do."

"So they will be gone soon? Before another meal?"

"I assume so. I would want to get moved in as early as possible, wouldn't you? I remember when this house was finally finished." She chuckled at the thought. "The very minute everything was moved in, I put the linens on our bed and climbed under the covers. It couldn't have been any later than five o'clock, and I got Horace to bring me some odds and ends for supper in bed. I was that determined to get off my feet."

"You were that tired?"

"Tired, yes, but mostly relieved. I had been longing for a cozy, comfortable home for so long that as soon as there was even a small piece of it I wanted to sink in and enjoy it for a good long while."

"When's the last time you took supper in bed?" Daisy asked with a grin. "Maybe you should do that for your next birthday."

"Oh, heavens, if you tell anyone that I took supper in

bed even *once*, I'll tell them your mind must be failing in your old age. Imagine what the tenants would think about such indolence!"

Daisy laughed, setting the now clean pan to the side before grabbing another plate. "We'll see. Maybe we can do it secretly now that I'm here to help run things."

Before Edith could respond there was a light knock on the doorframe.

"Excuse me. Mrs. Bennett?"

"Mrs. Watkins. How can I help?"

"I just wanted to let you know that our room is cleared out now. My husband and I will be on our way."

"Oh! Well, congratulations again. Let me walk you out." Edith nodded to Daisy, who stayed behind washing dishes as she walked with Mrs. Watkins. "Would you like to take some bread and cheese or something? Daisy can pack you a lunch so you have at least the semblance of a meal in your new home."

"No, thank you. I got Mrs. Jenkins to put together a meal to take for us."

"Well, then, I hope you enjoy it. I'll be able to return the overpayment for this month's board to your husband in a few days once I have gone to the bank. I'm so thrilled for you that the house was not delayed any longer."

"Oh, so am I," Mrs. Watkins said with visible relief. "It seems like Harold has been there twenty hours a day for the last week making sure the final details were handled. And with Mr. Chandler moving on to the inn, I suspect he wanted our job done as soon as he could."

The two women reached the parlor at the front of the house, where the door stood open. Edith could see

Jack Kinsey waiting with the wagon on the street, ready to drive them over before returning to his job at the livery. Mr. Watkins stood just inside the door, hands clasped behind his back.

"We've very much enjoyed having you," Edith said to them both. "I'm so thrilled for your house to be done, but if there's any reason you need another place to stay, or if you have any reason to refer a guest to me, I would appreciate it so much."

Mr. and Mrs. Watkins exchanged a look that Edith could not immediately interpret.

"Well . . ." he said.

"Harold, don't," his wife warned under her breath.

"What? Is something wrong?"

The couple exchanged another look, and Mrs. Watkins dropped her eyes to the floor.

"I'm not sure we'll be sending anyone your way in the immediate future," Mr. Watkins said stiffly.

"What? Why not? Please, if there's some way I can make it up to you—"

"No." He held up his hand to forestall her protests. "It's nothing you have done. Really almost nothing you could do differently. Over the several months we've stayed here you have been nothing but wonderful."

"Then . . . I'm sorry, but I don't understand what the problem could be."

He looked at his wife, and then back at Edith.

"It's that . . . captain," he said disdainfully.

Edith could almost hear the mocking in his tone at the man's insistence on others using his defunct title. Her heart dropped. That man had only ever been a nuisance since he moved in.

"What did he do?" she asked quietly.

"He is just . . ." Mr. Watkins frowned before saying primly, "He is simply not a gentleman. In all the time we lived here he has not said a word to my wife. At first I thought perhaps he was shy, or couldn't remember her name, but over time it has become clear that he frankly . . . I suspect he despises women in general. I have only seen him speak to myself or the two boys."

Edith kept quiet. She could not deny that everything the man was saying tallied with her own experience of Captain Stuart. She wasn't sure she'd ever seen him speak to Daisy at all, and she felt sure that any time he spoke to Edith herself it was strictly out of necessity and he wanted it over as quickly as possible.

"So, thank you, but if that man is still living here," Mr. Watkins continued, "we wouldn't want to put any of our friends in that situation."

"I understand completely. And thank you for telling me the truth."

They said their goodbyes, promising to see each other at church or the store in town someday soon. Edith was happy for the couple, setting out to begin their lives together in their new home that they had been dreaming out.

After the Watkinses had left, Edith made herself go upstairs to their room to give it a final check, just in case they had left something behind or something had been broken that she needed to take care of. When she stepped into the room, the faint scent of lemon verbena lingered. She walked slowly through the room, checking the interior of the chest of drawers and under the bed, but nothing seemed amiss. Mrs. Watkins had even stripped the bed of the soiled linens for her, so there was very little to do. Daisy could give the room a thorough cleaning before the end of the day and it would be ready for the next tenant whenever that happened.

But if Captain Stuart was driving business away, how long would Edith have to wait?

When she stepped back out into the hallway, she looked toward the door to the man's room. He had insisted on a room to himself, though his budget was not very large, so she had offered him the smallest available. Even now she regretted it; at the time she had thought that perhaps having a military man residing here would help the place feel more secure, but he had only been trouble.

Remembering that she had not yet seen him today, Edith crept up to his door and tried to listen, perhaps for movement, perhaps for snoring. For some indication that he was still in there and would be wanting breakfast soon, late though it was. She held her breath, pressing her ear to the door.

She heard murmuring, and a little movement. His voice was low, almost growling.

So, he was in there. Her tenants were not allowed to have guests without her knowledge, so she certainly hoped he was talking to himself, though she had to admit that if anyone were going to flaunt the rules it would be Mr. Stuart.

Edith pressed her ear harder, trying to understand what he was saying, but either the mumbling or the door was keeping her from comprehension.

She stepped away and headed back down to the kitchen. It was late enough that she would not have to feel bad about not holding breakfast for him—and besides, after her conversation with Mr. Watkins, Edith regretted ever making exceptions for the captain. Though she had never evicted a tenant in the ten years she had been running this boarding house, she had to admit the possibility was tempting. He was rude and uncouth and gave her the sense of bringing trouble to her door any minute.

If she had not just had a room emptied, she may be considering it more seriously.

Edith reached the bottom of the stairs into the parlor and resolved that she would think carefully about whether or not the money Bill Stuart added to her income was worth the hassle of him living there.

CHAPTER EIGHTEEN

The fundraising meeting at Mrs. Langdon's house went on far longer than Lillian had expected. So long, in fact, that the promotional committee did not get a chance to talk to the group at large about what they had discussed. It seemed to be accepted that they had not had a chance to do anything yet, and so instead the group's conversation revolved around possible dates and locations for the event.

By the time Lillian had said her final goodbyes and walked home, she was afraid she was going to be late helping Mary Ann make supper.

In fact, when she finally walked through the front door, she was surprised to see that her husband was home already. It was precisely times like this when Lillian felt guilty for having an occupation and interests outside the home. It felt as though every other woman in Juniper Falls would never dream of being out of the house when their husband arrived back.

"I'm so sorry I'm late," she called into the house,

hastily removing her hat and gloves. "Put me to work! Tell me what I can do to help."

She hurried into the dining room, where Ned was already seated at the head of the table, a cold glass of lemonade by his hand, condensation dripping slowly down the side. At a quick glance, Lillian noticed that the table had not been set yet, so she decided to start with that.

"And how was your day?" Ned asked kindly.

She opened the sideboard to pull out three plates and napkins. "I had that meeting today, remember?"

When she turned back around to the table, she saw that Ned was frowning, thinking. Lillian felt a stab of irritation that she was forever having to remind her husband details about her life. She even thought—uncharitably, she knew—that perhaps that was part of why he wanted so badly for her to resign from her job and stay home. So she would have fewer things going on in her life, fewer things he had to remember.

Lillian started setting the table, waiting for her husband's reaction.

"I'm sorry. My mind has been on inventory. I want to put in one last order before winter sets in, just in case the trains have trouble getting through."

She offered him a small smile before heading into the kitchen to see if Mary Ann needed any help.

"No, no," her sister said, waving her off. "Everything is just about done. Go ahead and sit down with Ned."

Mary Ann's unfailing competence in her domestic sphere never failed to make Lillian feel both grateful and a little ashamed of her own skills. She would need to do better if—when—Mary Ann eventually got married and left her. Perhaps honing those skills would be a good way to spend her final weeks before the new school year started.

But for now, she had more important things to worry about. Namely keeping Ned happy and taken care of. When she reentered the dining room, she sat at his left hand and apologized again.

"I'm sorry I'm late. I didn't think the meeting would go so long."

"It's fine," he said. "I remember that you told me, but could you remind me what meeting that was, please?"

She softened. He was trying. No one could be perfect all the time.

"It was with the committee to raise funds for the school. Mrs. Langdon. Mrs. Bennett. A few others."

"Didn't you just have a meeting with them last week?"

She looked at him with an unbelieving expression. "Well, yes, but you understand, I'm sure, that this is a process. This a huge endeavor. The concert we are planning includes several steps. There will likely be another meeting next week as well, since we want to get as many of the decisions made before classes start."

"Of course, before classes start."

Lillian might almost suspect her husband of sarcasm if she was not reasonably certain he had never spoken to her that way in all the years they had known each other.

"All right, here we are," Mary Ann said as she brought in the big cast-iron Dutch oven. The steam curled enticingly. Lillian could smell the subtle layers of beef, rosemary, carrot, and whatever other magic her sister put into the pot roast. "I was able to get a lovely, fat-marbled roast from Mr. O'Brien this morning, so I thought a treat would be in order, even if it did heat up the house a bit."

"It smells amazing," Lillian assured her. "You're my favorite sister."

Mary Ann laughed and gestured to Ned to say grace over the food. All conversation about Lillian's meeting ceased while they prayed, served supper, and settled in to eat—she didn't want to have to upset her husband unnecessarily, so she'd decided to let it drop—when her sister brought up the subject again.

"So, when I came in you were saying that you have a lot to do before classes start again?" Mary Ann said, cutting into a piece of potato.

"Oh. Um . . . yes. Right. So, classes start in four weeks, and the plan is to get as much set into place as we can by then . . ."

She continued on, relaying the details of the meeting and the committee's intention, even as with every sentence she felt more and more as though Ned could not care less about any of it. Her sister chimed in with questions and interest periodically, but the conversation felt rather flat with Ned so determined not to participate.

"Remember that Christmas concert they did back in Baltimore?" Mary Ann asked with a laugh. "You couldn't have been more than, what, fourteen?"

"Oh, my goodness, I completely forgot." Lillian blushed at the memory, despite the fact that it had happened more than ten years ago now. "How do you remember? You would have been . . . seven?"

"I barely remember it," Mary Ann explained to Ned,

"but I've heard the story enough times that it seems crystal clear."

"Do we have to?" Lillian laughed.

"As the story goes," Mary Ann continued, ignoring her sister's protests, "Lillian bravely and confidently signed up to recite a poem at the Christmas concert. She had a crush on one of the older boys and thought a Shakespeare sonnet would win him over."

"In my defense," Lillian interjected, "Shakespeare is always a good choice."

"Anyway, when the night came," Mary Ann said, "and her turn was announced, Lil got as far as two steps onto the stage before passing out completely."

"The stage lights were hot!"

"And she has never even been backstage at a theater since," her sister concluded.

Ned had watched the entire exchange with evident delight, learning about this side of his wife he had never seen. "So, then, I take it your role in this whole fundraising endeavor is *not* to perform?"

Lillian laughed again. "Absolutely not. Behind the scenes for me or nothing at all."

"I would think that, with that fear of being in front of crowds, you would not be so eager to return to teaching," Ned finally said, after finishing his last bite of supper.

Lillian was so struck by his deliberate, and somewhat heavy-handed, change of conversation topic that she was speechless for a moment. She could feel her sister's eyes on her, looking back and forth between Ned and Lillian.

"Ned . . ."

"No, this is enlightening." He leaned back in his

chair, as though inviting either one of the women to clear his plate.

Lillian felt angry and hurt, but also sad and disappointed, yet still desperate for connection and understanding, and she was completely overwhelmed by all of it. She had been teaching the entire four years they had been married, and before that as well, and it wasn't until she had gotten pregnant that her husband had even hinted that he did not want his wife to work. This was all new to their marriage, and she was at a loss as to how to handle it.

Lillian stood to clear the table, biting her tongue to keep the peace.

"You go on," Mary Ann whispered. "I can take care of this."

Lillian wanted to protest—Mary Ann should not be doing quite so much of the housework during these months that Lillian wasn't teaching—but she knew her sister was right. She and Ned needed to have a conversation, and if she did not force herself to do it, it might never happen.

She sat down again as Mary Ann silently cleared the table. It took her several trips to and from the kitchen, and this entire time neither Ned nor Lillian said a word to the other. The change in the whole mood of the meal was stark. Where was her supportive and kind husband?

Once they were truly alone again, Lillian took a deep breath.

"What changed?" she asked softly. She thought she already knew the answer but wanted to hear him say it. "You've never had a problem with me teaching before now."

He heaved a great sigh, as though she were asking something of him that he could not possibly be expected to provide but which he would somehow find the strength to do anyway. As though having an honest conversation with his wife were some enormous favor he was granting her.

"I was under the impression that you wanted a family with me," he said, his eyes boring into hers like a drill.

"I do, but—"

"I was also under the impression," he continued, not acknowledging that she had said anything, "that you got married in order to have a husband to care and provide for you."

She frowned. "I—I suppose, but—"

"So if both of those things are true, I simply cannot understand why you are insisting on continuing this occupation, continuing to stay on your feet, continuing to be so in the public eye that our neighbors must assume that my business is failing and you are forced to work to keep food on our table. You cannot deny that all that work must be a factor in losing our baby this spring."

Lillian almost laughed out loud at the absurdity but stopped herself in time. It was one thing for Ned to be concerned about her health after losing the baby. It was another thing entirely for Ned to try to control her choices because of what people in the town might or might not think, regardless of the truth.

For the first time, she realized that her husband's lack of confidence in himself was strongly affecting his choices. When they had first met, and when they were first making their plans to come West, he had seemed so excited about the fresh start and all the chances ahead of them. She saw now that maybe he was running away from something, instead of running to this new opportunity.

"I . . . I don't know what to say. I'm sorry if you think I am somehow bringing shame to you by . . . teaching."

Lillian had no idea what she could do to help this deep pain in Ned, and until he addressed it he would continue to lash out at her, blame her, continue to use whatever means he could to convince her not to return to her beloved position.

"I'm tired," she said finally, her voice breaking in the effort to hold back tears. "I've had a very long day and . . . I need to rest." She stood, pushing the chair into the dining table. "Excuse me."

She did not wait for a response. She did not look at him. She merely walked away, upstairs, where she could be alone.

CHAPTER NINETEEN

Being included on the fundraising committee for the school improvements seemed to have filled a need that Charlotte had not realized she had. When she and Mattie returned to the boarding house that night after the first meeting, she was full of stories and ideas and could not wait to tell her husband. Over the following few days, even more ideas had bubbled up. She felt cautiously optimistic that Juniper Falls would feel like home to them in no time at all.

But then, after the second meeting, when they had decided on the location and date for the Christmas concert, Charlotte realized she still had a long way to go before she would be accepted in this new town. It did not matter that she had hosted all manner of events for their church in Philadelphia. It did not matter that she had neither home nor children that needed her attention and thus could throw herself completely into planning.

All that seemed to matter to the women of Juniper

Falls was that she was a newcomer. That she did not understand the way things were done and so they did not yet trust her to do what was needed.

And few if any of them seemed inclined to take the time to explain any of it to her.

"Why don't we see if we can get a vocalist from Cheyenne to come sing?" she had suggested that afternoon at the second meeting. "They must have a larger arts community."

The chair of her committee on the event's location and decorations had pretended not to hear Charlotte.

Later she tried again. "Maybe we could hold it outdoors. Build a stage. A bright, sunny, winter afternoon?"

At least that time the woman next to her had acknowledged that she'd spoken. Still, her response felt just as harsh as no response at all. "Oh, no, we couldn't possibly, dear."

But no other details were forthcoming.

Maybe, Charlotte thought, she should just watch. Maybe that was what was expected of her. So, though she wanted nothing more than to jump in, to take on what needed to be done, to display her worth to these women, Charlotte kept her mouth closed, sat back in her chair, and listened. Ranchers' wives and frontier daughters were nothing like the friends and neighbors she had left back in Philadelphia. In the city, each row home shared walls with two others, the occupants practically on top of one another morning, noon, and night. Here in Juniper Falls, if she really wanted to, she could walk just a couple hundred yards outside the edge of town and scream as loudly as she could, and no one would hear her. In Philadelphia they could get almost anything they wanted quickly, but in the Wyoming Territory the cost and time to get something as simple as a piece of jewelry was prohibitive to most of these women.

Charlotte had only been in Juniper Falls for less than two weeks. She still had a long way to go before she truly understood what it meant to live in this wild, rugged landscape, let alone try to bring an element of civilization and the genteel the way these women were.

"I think we should have it at the Lantern Theater," Miss Wright said. "I know it's brand-new, but it has plenty of room, and the novelty is sure to bring in an audience."

Charlotte sat quietly, smug in her knowledge that Philadelphia was the home to the oldest theater in the nation. She almost wished she was back in that crowded city.

"We would have to pay the theater rental fee out of the money that is being raised," Mrs. Jarrett objected. "And that means that we either need to raise ticket prices or somehow put together a show that every man, woman, and child would want to come to, and . . ." She laughed awkwardly. "I'm not sure our students are up to that."

"Could the owner of the theater donate the space for one night?" Charlotte asked before she could stop herself. "Since this is a fundraiser?"

There was a moment of silence as all four faces turned toward her, expressions a mix of disbelief, pity, and amusement.

Mrs. Jarrett laughed again. "We are as like to get

Alexander Pike to preach a sermon Sunday morning while standing on his head as we are to get him to give away anything he can demand hard cash for. But then, I take it you haven't yet met him?"

Charlotte shook her head, a blush creeping up her neck. Once again, she had misread the situation in her new town.

"He is . . ." Mrs. Jarrett hesitated, searching for the word.

"He's not too *neighborly*," Miss Wright supplied, gently.

"That's probably the nicest way to say it," Mrs. O'Brien agreed.

"Oh." Charlotte felt small and silly. For the dozenth time that afternoon she wondered what she was doing there. "I see."

"I still think the theater is our best option," Miss Wright said. "The stage and the seats and lights are already there. The time and money we would save on having to decorate and outfit whatever other space we would use can be put back into whatever fee Pike charges us."

The conversation went on all around her while Charlotte kept her mouth shut. She had tried enough, and now had fully learned her lesson—they did not want her ideas. Though she was perfectly happy to slip into whatever role these women wanted of her, without some kind of guidance she had no idea what that might be. Even Mrs. Langdon, who had been so warm and welcoming at church a couple days earlier, was far too busy being hostess and committee chair to fill Charlotte in on the unspoken rules that she seemed to be breaking with every word out of her mouth.

As the women of her own committee continued to make plans, Charlotte watched her daughter across the room, evidently herself deep in planning.

Matilda, at least, seemed to care far less than Charlotte did. She sat in the corner with her friend Mrs. Frye, whispering and watching and altogether staying out of the way and out of the conversations. Matilda had always been able to find that line between making friends with seemingly no effort and not much caring what people thought of her. Charlotte had no idea where her daughter had gotten it—probably from her father.

So later that afternoon, when the two women returned to the boarding house in time for supper, she stayed quiet while Matilda told Henry and the others all about the meeting, what they were planning, and what she was looking forward to.

It wasn't until they were up in their room that night, getting ready for bed, that Henry asked Charlotte a question directly.

"You've been quiet," he said, unbuttoning his collar. "Did everything go all right today?"

Matilda was still downstairs, chatting with Jack and Silas, so Charlotte allowed herself to be honest.

"I suppose. I'm just feeling . . . lost." She sighed. "I don't know if I belong here."

"Really? You seemed to be taken under the wing of the pastor's wife the other day. And Mrs. Bennett invited you to join the committee in the first place. Neither of those things would have happened if you didn't belong."

"Oh, come now, Henry. Don't you think it's possible that they're all just being polite? One invitation and introduction does not mean anything beyond social niceties. Maybe coming out here was a mistake."

He peered at her. "You don't mean that, do you?"

"What else can it be?" She sat on the edge of the bed, feeling defeated. "First the hotel burns down, then it seems impossible to make any social inroads."

"Darling." He sat next to her and took her hand in his. "We've only been here a couple weeks. You have to give it at least a little time. Things will be better when the inn is finished, and when our life settles down a little bit."

"No, you don't understand . . ." In a few desperate sentences she described what had happened at the meeting earlier that day. "If we had the money to spare, I would almost want to pay whatever Mr. Pike's fee is myself, just to get these women to like me."

"Come now, darling," he said with a gentle smile. "You don't want to have to *buy* your way into society here, do you? Isn't that why we left Philadelphia? To live in a place where it doesn't matter what your grandfather earned?"

"Oh, yes," she retorted sarcastically. "The openness and opportunity is utterly overwhelming. From the sole option of sleeping in a boarding house to having each of my ideas dismissed at this meeting, I just cannot get enough of the *wealth* of possibilities."

Henry didn't respond, and when Charlotte looked back up at him, she could see that he was hurt.

"I'm sorry," she said, taking his hand. "I'm sorry,

darling. I didn't mean to snap at you. None of this is your fault. I know you're just trying to help."

He nodded.

"But please see," she continued, "that this is difficult for me. I'm not imagining the dismissals that I experienced today. I don't know what to do about it, and I'm not asking you to try to fix it. I just need you to hear me and sympathize."

"I do," Henry said softly. "You're right. I wasn't there. I'm sorry."

She sighed and flopped back, lying on the bed.

"I don't know what to do."

He lay at her side, her hand still in his. "If you figure it out and need my help, you know what to do."

"I do." She rolled over to her side and propped herself up on one elbow. "Thank you."

He pulled her roughly down on top of him, kissing the tip of her nose. "They'll see. Just you wait. Once those women give you a chance and see what you can do, you'll never be rid of them."

Charlotte laughed. Though she still felt lost, it was nice to know she still had a home with Henry.

CHAPTER TWENTY

With the location and date selected for the Christmas concert, Mattie and Lillian could begin their promotional efforts. It was still several months away, however, so there was no real hurry, and for several days after the second meeting, Mattie did not see her friend at all. She had even gone all the way to the Fryes' home to call on her, but had been turned away at the door. Mary Ann had been kind, but in a whisper told her that Lillian had been taken ill and was spending most of the time in bed.

"She'll be glad to know you called on her, though," the other woman assured her. "As soon as she is up and about, I'm sure she'll want to see you."

So Mattie needed to find something else to occupy her time. Though she gave brief thought to approaching the editor of the *Juniper Falls Gazette*, she knew that any request would be far better received when made by someone the man knew, or at the very least had met. She thought about seeing if Mr. Chandler and his team could use any help in rebuilding the inn, but feared she'd make the men uncomfortable by being the only woman there. Juniper Falls had a library and a theater and a church, but none of those seemed to be the thing she needed at that moment.

Instead, she left the Fryes' home and simply walked back toward the boarding house, stopping on the way to see if there had been any mail left for her or her parents.

When Mattie entered the general store, the familiar chime of the bell rang above the door. From where he stood at the counter measuring out some pounds of cornmeal for a young woman Mattie had not yet met, Mr. Thrush looked up and nodded his welcome to her. With as many times as she had come to check for mail, he not only knew her face quite well, but he also knew she was not likely to buy anything.

Maybe she would today, seeing as she had nothing else pressing to worry about.

But when she walked to the back of the store, where Mr. Quinn's mail and telegraph desk sat, the expression on his face when he saw her sent all other thoughts far away.

"Miss McBride!" he said excitedly, already diving down behind his counter to find something. "I have mail for you. I almost thought to go find you at Mrs. Bennett's, before I reminded myself that you're here nearly every day anyway. The mail came yesterday, and both you and your parents have received something. Here, let me see . . ."

Mattie almost didn't hear the rest of what he had said after the words *I have mail for you.* It was true she had checked in nearly every day in the two weeks since her family had arrived in Juniper Falls—just long enough to get used to the disappointment of leaving empty-handed.

Mr. Quinn handed over two letters, one a fat, official-looking envelope addressed to her father with a return address in New York City, the other a worn, thinner missive addressed in Duncan's familiar handwriting to *Miss Mattie McBride*. She felt her whole body soften just at the sight.

"Thank you! Oh, Mr. Quinn, I can't tell you what this means to me."

He chuckled. "None of my doing, but I am happy for you. Go on, now, and read the thing you've been waiting weeks for. I expect to see you back here in another couple days with another letter to send out."

She clutched the mail to her chest, these few precious, irreplaceable sheets of paper, as she walked back out through the general store to the busy main street. Mr. Quinn's words had reminded her that Duncan had to have written this letter before he received her last one. She had written him a couple times over the weeks that they were traveling to Juniper Falls, but this was the first letter she had received from him.

She was bursting with excitement wondering what he would have to tell her, and she hurried back to the boarding house so she could have a chance to read it in privacy. She ran up the stairs, ignoring Daisy's greeting, and was thrilled to find both of her parents out. After closing the bedroom door behind her, she kicked off her boots and settled in.

Dearest Mattie, the letter began.

She had curled up in her small cot, her knees up to

her chest, hugging herself with one arm while she held his letter in the other. Tears stung her eyes as she finally, for the first time since leaving Philadelphia, allowed herself to fully recognize just how much she missed him. Up till now she had simply put it out of her mind, looking for anything to distract her from such difficult feelings.

I'm writing this four days after you got on the train leaving Philadelphia, the letter continued. *Four days and three hours and eleven minutes, to be exact. I miss you so much, but I'm trying not to let myself think about it (which I'm sure you are doing the same), since we don't know how long it will be until we see each other again. I'm sure it will not surprise you to learn that I have done nothing but think about when we will be together again. I've walked the streets where we have been. I've been to the park where we got caught out in the rain. I've visited the central market and even eaten some of Mrs. Belmont's taffy that you love so much. Anything to feel close to you, my love.*

The business at the store remains steady. My brother has offered to come for an extended visit to help out more, as I feel stretched quite thin. My father's health remains poor, but consistently so, and I have no more idea of when I will be able to take the next step than I did when you left. I'm so sorry, my love. I miss you dreadfully and wish I had better news to offer you.

I will tell you this, however. I've been thinking, and after being here by myself for a few days, have realized that I want to see more of the world. I've lived in Philadelphia my entire life and never ventured any farther than Baltimore, and now you are nearly two thousand miles away, with so many exciting stops and stories in between us.

So, if it is all right with you, when my biggest commitment here is at an end, I would like to follow you to Juniper Falls. I'm certain I can rely on my brother to look after the shop on his own for a few months, and I am equally certain it would break your mother's heart if I sent for you to come back and be married in Philadelphia. This way I can see more of our beautiful country, your parents can be present when we are wed, and you can have at least a few weeks longer with them before we return.

I know it may seem like an unnecessary expense, but to me there is nothing I would rather spend our money on than being with family and enjoying seeing more of our great country. Won't it be far more exciting (and safer) to take the train back east together, rather than you doing it by yourself?

Write to me as soon as you can to tell me what you think of this plan. Though we don't know yet when I will be able to come out, I would like to have everything planned and ready for that eventuality.

This letter is short, I know. I'm sorry for that, but I want to send it right away. As soon as I had the idea, I longed to share it with you and hear your response. I would have telegraphed if it were less expensive to tell you that I miss you a hundred times. I'm sorry if you had to wait long for this communication. I'm sorry I can't be there in person to tell you I miss you. But I promise to make both things up to you as soon as we are once again breathing the same air.

All my love.

Yours,

Duncan.

Mattie closed her eyes and rested her forehead against her knees, overwhelmed with the love and hope that she felt after receiving this letter. He missed her and he loved her and he was thinking months in advance about how to see her again. And he wanted to come *here*!

She could not wait to show him around Juniper Falls, to introduce him to her new friends. She had a feeling Mr. Quinn in particular would love to meet this man about whom she had so much talked.

Her trunk sat at the foot of her cot, and she opened it immediately to dig out her paper and writing desk to respond to him.

Belovedest Duncanest darling, she wrote. *I love your plan. I wish you could get on a train to me right this second (though I know better). Juniper Falls will only be more dear to me if I get to share it with you as well.*

Let me tell you about the latest news from yours truly. You'll never guess. Mrs. Frye and I are angling to be interviewed by one of the local reporters . . .

CHAPTER TWENTY-ONE

A few days had passed since the Watkinses had moved out and Edith had yet to fill their room with new boarders, but having fewer people to feed and clean up after was a nice trade for the loss of income. Ever since she had opened her boarding house, the fluctuation in funds had been a cause of worry. It was still plenty early in the season, however. Most newcomers to any frontier town, their little Juniper Falls included, arrived in the autumn, before the snow fell and after a long summer of travel. If she had not yet filled that vacancy by the end of October, *then* she would worry about making her budget stretch through the winter. But at the moment there were plenty of other things to be thinking of.

She had volunteered to be on the food and drink committee for the Christmas concert, and simply trusted that the funds she would need for that would be available when December came around. Though she had given more thought to asking Bill Stuart to leave, she knew she could not afford to have a second room sit empty. The situation was even more pressing with each update she received from the McBrides about the inn's reconstruction. Surely they too would be moving out in the next couple of months, and then Edith would really need to hustle to find boarders.

In the meantime, she kept her morning busy with all the laundry to do, bread to bake, weeding to make headway on, and any number of other chores to keep the place running and comfortable for those still under her roof.

She had just been about to sit down for a quiet break in her afternoon before she had to start supper when Mr. McBride came down the stairs and found her in the dining room.

"Mrs. Bennett, do you have a moment? I wonder if we could talk about how much longer my family and I will need to be staying here with you."

All thoughts of her needed break dissipated. "I'm happy to. I was just about to make myself some tea. Why don't I brew us both some and I'll meet you in the parlor?"

He nodded and went to go wait while she managed to find the energy to serve yet another person that day. But, she reminded herself, this was her job. This was what her life was about. She could take a break after supper, once everyone was in bed again.

Ten minutes later, Edith carried a tray laden with cups, sugar and cream, and tea into the parlor. She set it carefully on the table in the middle of the room and served her guest and herself while inquiring after his health.

"Oh, fine, fine," he said, watching her pour the tea.

"The inn is coming along. We're getting to know Juniper Falls. I feel like I can take a truly deep breath for . . . maybe the first time in my life."

"Really? Did you grow up in Philadelphia?"

She handed him his tea.

"I did. My family came over from England less than a century ago and pretty much didn't move from the spot where they first settled. I haven't known anything but cobblestone streets and hired hansom cabs."

"This must feel very different."

"It does." He fell quiet for a moment as if lost in thought. "More than you probably can guess."

She spooned a little sugar into her tea and sat back in her chair, letting Mr. McBride lead the conversation.

"As you know," he began after clearing his throat, "Ralph Chandler and his boys were able to get to work on the inn nearly as soon as we arrived in town. Your own and Mr. Bullock's advice was invaluable."

"I'm so happy for you," she said sincerely. "It truly is such a blessing that Mr. Chandler was available right away."

"*And* that you had available space here," he added, nodding. "Anyway, we got a contingent, preliminary promise of payment from the insurance company, since Mr. Bullock was kind enough to start that for us. Though nothing is certain, it seems we will have the resources necessary to finish the inn well before winter sets in, though I can't say for certain how long. I know you were not expecting to have us here, so I wanted to check with you if we need to press Mr. Chandler to work faster."

"Oh, no. Heavens! No, don't worry about that at all.

I have the space, easily. You can stay as long as you like. Though, of course, I do hope for your sake that everything is taken care of promptly."

"Thank you. We do, too, of course." He sipped his tea. "But it is also very helpful that we don't have to worry about being a nuisance here. I'm certain that you don't realize how much you've helped us. Coming up to us in the street that first day was a stroke of luck on our side."

Edith basked in his praise, proud of her role in the community and the way she had been able to step in and fill the need presented. The longer she lived in Juniper Falls the more she was proud of her place in it.

But something Mr. McBride had said raised questions for her.

"You mentioned that the promise of payment from the insurance company was only contingent . . . ?"

"Yes." He sighed and put down his teacup. "Since there was no one in the building, and no direct testimony identifying the cause of the fire, they need to eliminate the possibility that I committed arson in an attempt to receive a fraudulent payout."

"Oh no!"

"I can understand their point of view. The ink on the document was practically still wet when the fire occurred. To my knowledge, they have been in contact with Sheriff Sands here, as well as Mr. Bullock, and I'm hopeful that it will all be resolved soon."

Edith suddenly remembered Sheriff Sands visiting her the previous week, and all his questions about the McBrides themselves. She wondered how much of the investigation Mr. McBride was aware of. Had the sheriff spoken to the man directly?

"Oh . . . yes, let's hope. Have you heard anything more about what the sheriff has found?"

"Nothing, no. Hopefully that means there's nothing to find."

"Yes." Edith sipped her tea, keeping her thoughts to herself. "Well, as I say, it's no problem for you all to stay as long as you like. I know firsthand how easy it is for plans to fall apart."

He retrieved his tea again and sipped it as well, looking around the room.

"You know," he said after a moment. "I wonder if there's one other thing I could ask of you."

"Of course. Whatever I can do to make your stay here and your transition to Juniper Falls easy."

He cleared his throat and leaned forward to set his now empty cup back on the tray. When he sat back up, his expression seemed to be one of embarrassment.

"I wonder if you might . . . Well, no, let me . . . I'm sorry." He laughed. "I'm not quite sure what I'm even asking for."

Edith waited, sipping her tea and giving the man a moment to think.

"As I said, I am not sure you recognized how much you've been able to help us, and I'm so sorry, but I wonder if I could ask for just one more favor."

"Oh? Oh. Well, yes, probably. If I can help, I'm happy to."

"Inviting my wife to that fundraising committee meeting was so . . . kind. It's exactly the kind of thing she had hoped to be part of when we decided to buy the inn here. If we had been able to settle into our new home immediately as we'd expected, she might have very well started her own committee for something or other by now. But I'm afraid the adjustment to frontier life and to these new people has been more difficult for her than she anticipated."

"What do you mean?"

"Oh, nothing terrible. Nothing even specific, that I can tell. And please, maybe don't tell her that I asked this of you. It would embarrass her terribly." He folded his hands in his lap.

Edith smiled to herself at the idea of this sweet man trying to help his wife without her knowing.

"She is trying so hard to be available and be what these women need, and I think perhaps she doesn't understand quite what that is."

"So . . . Mrs. McBride needs me to . . . what? Soften the transition?"

"Something like that. Maybe you could go with her to a future meeting? Or maybe you could host some of the women here for something and include my wife? I'm sorry, I'm not certain what all women do when men are not around."

Edith offered him an understanding smile. "I can come up with something. I'm so sorry that Mrs. McBride doesn't feel at home here like she'd hoped. How is your daughter doing with all of this?"

"Mattie? Oh, she's grand. She always is. Could find a friend at the North Pole, that one. I think her biggest concern right now is when she will see her beau again, but I have no doubt she will be perfectly fine until whenever that happens. No, I'm not worried about Mattie."

Edith nodded; the young woman did seem to be tarred with a very different brush than her mother.

"I'm happy to do what I can for you wife as long as you all are here, and later than that if needed. I'll just have to have a think on what that might be."

"And of course," Mr. McBride said, "once we have our place, if there's anything we can do for you, I'm sure we'd be happy to." He stood, signaling that he had nothing more to address with her. "Please tell me how we can help."

The front door opened abruptly, slamming backward into the wall. Edith winced, wondering if the handle had dented her plaster, as Bill Stuart tore inside and up the stairs without so much as glancing at either person in the parlor. Though she knew it had nothing to do with her, Edith was embarrassed on the man's behalf that he had behaved so in front of Mr. McBride.

Edith picked up the tray with the ends of their tea and stood as well. "Thank you, Mr. McBride. If all my tenants were as understanding as you all have been, I would never have a stressful day in my life."

CHAPTER TWENTY-TWO

If it had not been August and Lillian had been expected at school all week, she never would have allowed herself to loll about in bed for several days, telling Ned that she was sick. Letting her sister make excuses for her. Usually she had a very strong sense of responsibility and prided herself on never missing a deadline. But in times like this, she was grateful for her summer off work, grateful for her sister to take care of the home, grateful that she could give herself the time and space to simply be sad for a few days.

She felt as though she was grieving what she'd thought her marriage was—who she'd thought her husband was. He had been so encouraging and supportive and proud of her career as a schoolteacher, but she realized now that he had only been waiting for it to be over. As though he could afford to be generous, knowing that he could wait her out.

If Lillian was a spiteful person, she'd insist on never

getting pregnant so she could maintain her employment that Ned had made her believe he valued.

There was a light knock on the door, and when Lillian called out, Mary Ann stuck her head in.

"How are you feeling? Mattie is at the door again, but I can tell her you're still feeling sick. I've already turned her away once."

"I'm not sick," she mumbled.

"What's that?"

Lillian forced herself to sit up. "I'm not sick. I'm just . . . I can come down. Give me a few minutes to put myself together."

Mary Ann looked at her sadly. "If you're sure . . ."

"I am. I should have gotten up yesterday. I'll be down as soon as I can."

Mary Ann nodded and closed the door gently, leaving her alone.

When Lillian had finally gotten dressed, finally washed her face and combed her hair for the first time in a few days, she had to admit that she felt somewhat better. Her heart was still broken by the revelation about her husband, and her energy was nowhere near what she'd hoped for, but at least she could interact with another person and not fall completely to pieces.

She needed to. She needed this. She needed to try to look forward with this new context.

And she hoped that her friend Mattie—who was always lively, always chipper, always curious—would be just the person to help her do that.

"Mattie," she said as she came down the stairs. "Thank you for calling."

Her friend stood at the entrance, a concerned look

on her face. Lillian had to assume that Mary Ann had offered Mattie a seat, but the latter seemed reluctant for some reason. When she saw the look on Mattie's face change into one of relief and hope, Lillian felt a little guilty for making her friend worry.

"I don't have to stay long," Mattie said as Lillian joined her. "If you need to rest more, I just wanted to say hello."

"No, no. I'm all right. Come sit."

The two women made themselves comfortable in the sitting room, where Mary Ann had brought a small plate of cookies.

"Can Mary Ann get you coffee? Tea? I'm sure we have something," Lillian said.

"No, no. Thank you. But tell me how you're feeling. Did your sister tell you I visited yesterday too?"

"I think so . . ." Lillian wasn't ready to admit how much of the last couple days she could not remember, buried as she was under the thick quilt of sadness. "I'm sorry for making you worry. We didn't have any plans that I forgot, did we?"

Mattie laughed. "I always have plans of some kind, but no, you didn't forget anything. I'm glad you're feeling better."

Lillian smiled weakly. She didn't like feeling deceitful, but letting Mattie think she had been ill was far preferable to the reality.

"Thank you. But how are you?"

"Oh!" Mattie lit up. "Guess what! I finally heard from Duncan."

As the other woman went on and on about her beau and their plans, Lillian tried to focus on her words, to drum up her excitement for Mattie, and to not let any of her own disillusionment about her marriage and her husband cloud her thinking.

"So even though that's probably not going to be anytime soon," Mattie concluded, "at least I have it to look forward to."

"That's wonderful. Really. I can't wait to meet him."

"Thank you." She beamed. "But in the meantime, I have to find something else to fill my time. Have you thought any more about us going to talk to the editor of the paper? What was his name?"

"Mr. Sharp. No, I hadn't thought about it, but you're right that it sounds smart. I only know him by reputation, though."

"Then maybe we should start sooner rather than later," Mattie said with a grin.

"What do you mean?"

She stood up. "Let's go now! I mean, of course, if you're feeling well enough. You should definitely go back to bed if you're still sick. But if we need to both meet *and* charm Mr. Sharp, as well as being interviewed and allowing time for whatever kind of articles about the Christmas concert he will write, maybe we should start now."

Lillian laughed. "It's August!"

Mattie shrugged. "If this idea about the paper doesn't work, isn't it better we know now?"

Lillian had never had a friend like Mattie, one who barreled forward despite any number of hurdles. Lillian herself allowed even the hint of an obstacle to slow her down. Being friends with someone like Mattie was exciting while also being a little scary. She couldn't help thinking about what Ned would say about her forwardness if he learned she was planning on simply walking into the office of the *Juniper Falls Gazette* to ask for a favor from a stranger.

But if she let herself think about her husband too long she might fall apart completely.

Lillian stood. "All right. Yes. Let me tell Mary Ann where I'll be, and then we can go . . . give it a try, I guess."

Twenty minutes later the two women were walking through the Fryes' neighborhood on their way to the main street of Juniper Falls.

"I have actually been in the newspaper office once," Lillian confided in Mattie. "When Ned wanted to place an advertisement for his store. But I only spoke to one of the other men setting the type there briefly, and handed over the envelope that Ned had given me. I saw Mr. Sharp from afar, and he comes to church once every few months, but otherwise I'm walking in as blindly as you are."

"Well . . ." Mattie began thoughtfully. "Maybe our ignorance will be a blessing. Maybe he's the kind of man who likes to talk about himself."

"Or maybe we will inadvertently offend him by mentioning something that everyone else knows not to."

"Hey, now, don't think like that," Mattie said. "We are two kind and charming young women who are doing something for the community. He'll love us."

Lillian smiled. "Where do you get such optimism?"

"I'm not sure. Maybe a defense against all my older siblings? Maybe a way for me to ignore all the boring bits of my life? Who's to say? "

They reached Main Street and turned east, passing only three storefronts before finally arriving at the office of the *Juniper Falls Gazette*.

"I'll do the talking," Lillian said. "At least at first. They'll know my face."

When the two women entered the office they found one man, a few years older than them, hunched over a desk near the front of the room. At the very back of the room was what looked to be a printing press, with a slightly older man leaning over fiddling with something on the machine.

Lillian cleared her throat, and the younger man looked up.

"Can I help you?"

"We, um . . . we were wondering—hoping, really . . . Actually, I should start with, we're here representing the —um, school? And we, um . . ."

She looked to Mattie for help. Her thoughts felt scattered and she didn't know what part of their request to start with, nor even how to introduce themselves.

"I'm sorry," Mattie said with a winning smile. "We're just so excited."

The man had stood by now and come to meet them near the door, his hands in his trouser pockets as he watched Lillian stumbling. He chuckled at Mattie's frankness.

"Why don't you ladies take a seat and we can get to the bottom of this."

In moments, they were settled in narrow chairs that sat opposite the man's desk. He had introduced himself as Mr. Jeffrey Nolan, a reporter; Lillian had recognized his name from her husband's store records.

"I'm the only other full-time person, besides Sharp back there." Mr. Nolan gestured to the older man in the back of the office, who thus far had not acknowledged the women's entrance at all. "So why don't you tell me or ask me what you came for, and then we can see what needs to be done."

Lillian and Mattie exchanged a look, and the younger woman nodded encouragingly at her. Now that they were here, now that this man was being so kind, Lillian felt more settled and more in possession of her faculties.

"Well, as I said—or maybe I didn't—Miss McBride and I are here on behalf of the fundraising committee for the Juniper Falls Primary School."

He nodded, listening carefully.

"We will be putting on a Christmas concert in December, with all the proceeds going to pay for a new coat of whitewashing and new trees for the school grounds, and the two of us are on the promotional committee."

"We *are* the promotions committee," Mattie interjected.

"Ah, I see," he said, leaning back in his chair. "And so you thought the newspaper would be an ideal partner for you to help get the word about."

"Yes!" Mattie said excitedly. "Precisely. You are in the business of spreading news, are you not? Can we count on your help?"

Mr. Nolan looked back at Mr. Sharp, who still had paid them no mind.

"It's not up to me, you understand," he said with a grin. "But I'd love to help if I can. Why don't we meet at the cafe for coffee and pie in, say, three days' time, and you can tell me all about it."

He stood and glanced back at Mr. Sharp again. It was clear to Lillian that he needed to get back to work.

"Thank you," she said, standing as well. "We'd love that. We're very grateful. Thank you so much."

"Don't thank me yet. But I look forward to continuing this conversation. Thank you, ladies."

CHAPTER TWENTY-THREE

Charlotte sat alone at the dining room table in Mrs. Bennett's boarding house, going over her list for the third time. The burned-out inn had been under construction for just over a week, and much of the money they had been loaned to cover the cost had drained from their bank account with alarming speed. Though she'd hoped the spending would probably slow, all those supplies needed to be purchased right away. The McBrides were still waiting to hear about the next step from the insurance company, after the small contingent payment, and if that didn't happen soon, they may need to halt the building, ask for more favors, or come up with some miracle of finding the money needed. She murmured to herself as she added up the columns of numbers in the ledger again, checking that her math was right. It was going to be a stretch, but she thought they could make it all work. Especially if the full insurance payout came soon.

When the McBrides had lived in Philadelphia,

Henry had been one of many—*many*—lawyers in the city. He'd had a solid reputation, and his clients never left him, but there were so many other men practicing the same trade that throughout the almost thirty years they had been married it felt as though they were never able to get ahead. In their moments of penny-pinching, she knew Henry daydreamed about a different occupation in which he could not have to worry about every billable hour, and even get outdoors once in a while. He downplayed his concern, but more than once Henry had made a joke about going blind from so many nights at his desk with just a lantern. Later, when all their children but Matilda had moved out to homes of their own, both Henry and Charlotte realized that if they wanted to give themselves one final adventure they would need to do it soon.

Charlotte had always taken care of their home and children as well as their finances, leaving Henry free to focus on just his work. When they chose to come west to the Wyoming Territory and embark on an entirely new business, there seemed to be no reason to change things. In Philadelphia, he'd trusted her to budget as needed and to let him know if he should look for additional clients. Here, there was no way for him to earn money to add to their accounts. She would just have to pull the purse strings a little tighter until they opened the inn.

Now that they were getting settled in Juniper Falls, there were so many other things to think about. Finishing rebuilding the staircase was only the first step. If the construction on the inn was really going to be completed in the next month or two, that meant that they should have ordered replacement furniture weeks ago. It was just one more task that was added to her pile of things to worry about that she wasn't expecting when they came west.

Charlotte closed her eyes and tried to envision what the completed hotel would look like, how it would feel, what they would do to welcome their guests.

Beds for each room. Requisite linens, and extras for laundry days. A chest of drawers for each room. A washstand, with bowl and pitcher. Towels. Not to mention everything else, from rugs, curtains, and chamber pots to vases, wallpaper, art to hang, coffee cups, and so much more. They wanted to—eventually—be a location to host parties and receptions, which would require an entirely different layer of outlay for items like champagne glasses or serving trays. When she and Henry had begun discussing this adventure, Charlotte had had a vision in her mind of what their inn would look like, what it would feel like, what kind of guests it would attract.

There was a long road between here and there.

A road paved with mountains of expenses.

She sighed, set down her pencil, and leaned back in her chair.

She had heard from Mr. Chandler that there were a handful of pieces on the upper floors that might be salvageable, but he suggested that the scent of burnt wood might make them less than desirable. Perhaps they would have to go in the McBrides' private rooms.

Today she would go to the site of the inn to assess what all they had to work with and what they still needed. She would check it against her list. She would check what money they had left in the bank account.

And she would make the necessary decisions.

As she was sitting there alone, she heard footsteps coming down the stairs. Soon after, Mrs. Bennett was standing in the doorway to the dining room.

"Oh, I didn't realize you were here. Do you need anything, Mrs. McBride? I can make you some tea or find a snack if you're hungry."

"No, thank you. Is it all right that I'm sitting here? I can get out of your way if you need me to. I just needed something that felt like a desk so I could spread all of this out."

"What are you working on?" Mrs. Bennett sat down across the table from her.

"Figuring out what we still need to buy and where on earth we are going to find the money to do so." She sighed. "I really thought all of this would be so much easier."

She leaned forward, elbows on the table and head resting in her hands. She could feel the other woman watching her. She hated to be seen as vulnerable in this moment, but she was so tired and so dejected she could not bring herself to much care. Though it was just a boarding house, this was her home—at least for now— and she needed to be able to be herself here.

"You know," Mrs. Bennett began, "if you're available in a few days, I was wondering if I could ask for your help."

Charlotte looked up abruptly. The idea that this well-established, capable woman would need her help with anything was frankly laughable, not to mention surprising. But when she saw Mrs. Bennett's expression, she noticed the uncertainty. And no matter what else could be said about Charlotte McBride, she was nothing if not confident in the things that she attempted, or she didn't attempt them at all.

"I'm happy to, of course. What is it you need help with?"

"It's my turn to host our quilting circle. Just maybe eight or nine women from church who come together for one afternoon each month to sew together patch-work squares."

"Oh, that sounds lovely. I'm afraid I don't have any of my quilting supplies out of the trunks, though. I'm not sure how I can help."

"Trust me, just one extra pair of hands and eyes is exactly what I need. Daisy will stay in the kitchen preparing the lunch, and I will find myself going back and forth to serve food. Probably find an additional lamp when Mrs. Gilpin's eyes begin to strain. All kinds of things. But if I could trust you to sit in the parlor with the women and help them feel at home, that would be a weight off my mind."

"I'm not sure . . . What if I helped Daisy serve and you stayed out here with your guests?"

Mrs. Bennett chuckled. "I've tried that before, too, and I always end up having to get up to look for this or that because I can't quite remember or can't quite describe how to find it. Plus, you know, I was hoping it would be a good opportunity for you to get to know some of the other women more."

Other than attending church last Sunday morning and occasionally visiting the general store, Charlotte had not really interacted with the women of Juniper Falls since the most recent fundraising meeting. She was never one to back down, and hated to give up, but at the same time she felt like she was missing . . . *something*. That indefinable quality that had helped her slip into a new group so often before.

"I don't know . . ."

"I will be here the whole time, and if you really feel like it's too much on the day then we can find another path."

"Are you just doing this because you feel sorry for me?"

"Oh, heavens. Not at all. The help in hosting is what I have been missing all the previous times it has been my turn. It's just lucky for me that you happen to be living here right now and I can trust you to be charming and welcoming. There was—" She stopped herself and grinned a little guiltily. "I probably shouldn't say this, so keep it to yourself. There was a couple here about a year ago, and I didn't even tell the woman that this quilting event was happening, in hopes that she would make other plans that afternoon. No, Mrs. McBride, I promise that if my invitation helps you at all, that is simply a bonus. You are going to be wonderful at running your inn. You have precisely the right temperament."

"Will Mrs. Langdon be there?"

"She's invited, of course, though she doesn't always have the time. I'm sure you can imagine how busy she is as the pastor's wife."

Charlotte nodded and pursed her lips. "Well . . . all right. If you're sure I won't embarrass you."

"I'm sure. And besides, all these women know each

other and will be occupied with putting together the quilt, so there will likely be very little pressure for you to talk if you don't want to. It will be on August twenty-fifth, everyone arriving about midmorning, after breakfast, and staying through midafternoon. Feeding all those women will keep Daisy and myself plenty busy."

"Thank you for inviting me."

"Thank *you* for helping me. Now." Mrs. Bennett stood again, resting her palms on the table. "If you're sure you don't need a snack, hopefully you won't mind my getting one. I'll leave you to your ledgers."

Charlotte smiled and waved her away, lost in her thoughts.

CHAPTER TWENTY-FOUR

Leaving the newspaper office with Lillian that afternoon, Mattie felt like she had put down another tiny little root here in Juniper Falls. She was on the committee to make something happen, and they were taking steps toward their goal, and she had met someone knew who would then recognize her if they ran into each other at the general store, and on and on. She beamed as she walked back to the boarding house after saying goodbye to her friend; that joy infused much of her following days. She would be so excited to show Duncan around the town whenever he was able to come out West.

If she also worried about pulling up such roots when Duncan Shaw came to marry her, Mattie didn't allow that concern to show in her face or her actions. Every day they were in Juniper Falls she worked toward settling in, making friends, and creating a home and community for her family. She wished her brothers and sister could be here too.

For the next several days she lived in a cloud of anticipation. Despite the initial setbacks of their arrival in this town, Mattie felt as though she had so much to look forward to: Duncan visiting (eventually), being interviewed by the newspaper, choosing all the decorations and fun little details of the new hotel. She almost hated to have to go to sleep each night for fear of missing something exciting.

That Sunday after church, she returned to the boarding house with her parents and had filled them both in on Duncan's plans to come out to the territories to marry her. She could tell her mother was not looking forward to Mattie leaving to go back East eventually, but on the surface she seemed all support and love.

"Well, the next time you write to him," she said as they entered the parlor, "you tell Duncan that we can't wait to see him. You all can get married in the lobby of our finished hotel. We'll make it a big party."

"Thanks, Mama." Mattie kissed her mother's cheek. "I'm going to go write him now, actually."

"Don't be too long. Mrs. Bennett will have lunch ready for us any minute."

With promises to be back down in the dining room soon, Mattie ran upstairs, eager to write to Duncan all about a funny little moment that had happened at church that morning.

When she reached their room, Mattie sat down on the edge of her cot. Over the couple of weeks that they had been in Juniper Falls, she had gotten more used to sleeping in the cramped area. When Mr. and Mrs. Watkins had moved out of the boarding house, there was a small part of Mattie that hoped her parents would rent that room, too, so she could sleep in a proper bed.

But she knew, without them even saying, that money was tight. Rebuilding and refurnishing the inn was far beyond what the McBrides had expected when they arrived in the Wyoming Territory. And so, instead, she just counted herself grateful that her parents were providing her this bed and this opportunity at all.

She was alone in the room now, at least.

Mattie leaned down and reached under the cot, where she had stored her personal items. She had brought with her from Philadelphia a small cigar box, inside of which she kept some of the small things that held big memories for her. When her parents had told her about the plan to come west to Wyoming, they had insisted that she limit her belongings to what would fit in a single chest. At first, she had been heartbroken over the thought of having to get rid of her childhood dollhouse and old diaries, but when Duncan heard the news he offered to store them for her. In his basement was another entire trunk of her belongings, including the towels and blankets she'd been stitching for years to fill her hope chest. Whenever she saw him again she would also be reunited with her lifetime of belongings. In the meantime, she had this small, manageable collection to harken back to some of her happiest days. She sighed happily as she opened the box and saw what was inside.

"What's that?" her mother asked as she entered the bedroom. "Doesn't look like you're writing. I came up to tell you lunch is served."

Mattie looked up. "I got distracted thinking about all the things I left behind at his house."

"Ah, yes. It was lovely of him to offer that space. But

you didn't answer me . . . What is in the box? I don't think I've seen it before."

"Oh, just a little collection of odds and ends. Things that remind me of back home, or Duncan, or when I was a child."

"Souvenirs?"

"Something like that."

"Can I see?"

Mattie brought the box over to where her mother stood, and together they sat side by side on the edge of the bed. Holding the box carefully, she lifted the lid to examine what was inside. The scent of dried roses wafted up, taking her back to her days with Duncan. The first thing on top was a ticket stub. She handed it to her mother.

"This was the show that Duncan and I saw the night he asked me to marry him," she said in a soft voice. "And this ribbon . . ." She pulled out a dark green hair ribbon that had settled along the length of the box. "This was the first thing Duncan ever gave me, when we were thirteen years old."

"I remember that. You came home absolutely flushed. I thought you were sick, until you explained where you had been. I knew that day that I would never be able to separate you two."

Mattie laughed. "I didn't realize he was even paying attention to me until that day."

"What about this?"

Her mother picked up a dried rose.

"That is from the first time Duncan left me flowers as a surprise on our front steps. He'd brought me flowers before, but always when we were to spend the afternoon together. This was just a small surprise out of the blue."

"That boy is so thoughtful. What about this button? It doesn't look familiar at all."

"Oh, I had forgotten about that." She picked up the brown mother-of-pearl button and held it in her open palm, close to her face to look at it carefully. "Do you remember those first few days we were here, and I went over to the inn to try to shift some things around and get a head start on cleaning up the place? When I moved aside some of the more heavily charred wood, I found this button wedged partway under the baseboard. It doesn't seem like it has any fire damage, so I'm not sure how it got in there. I thought maybe I'd keep it as a reminder of the fire and all that we had to deal with when we got here. But I've been so distracted with Lillian and the fundraising committee and Duncan's letters that I forgot all about it."

"Will you throw it out?"

Mattie pursed her lips in thought. "Not right away. Maybe once I'm back in Philadelphia and the inn isn't part of my daily life, I won't care about being reminded of it. We'll see."

"And in the meantime, it doesn't take up too much room."

"Right. Plus, I'm kind of proud of how much work I did to clean up that place."

She put the ticket stub, dried flower, and other items back in the cigar box. Closing the lid, Mattie stood to put the box back under her bed.

Suddenly, her mother seized her wrist, stopping Mattie from putting the box away.

"What's wrong?"

"I just had a thought. It might be nothing, and I don't want to— Do you trust me?"

"Um." Mattie's mind was going in several different directions at once, she was so confused about this abrupt shift in the conversation. "Yes, but . . . what's wrong?"

"Will you let me take that button?"

"The one I found in the inn?"

She dug it out of the box again and held it up between them. Her mother held out an open palm and Mattie dropped the button in it.

"Mama, what is going on?"

"Tell me again exactly where and how you found it."

"Not until you tell me why."

"Well . . . I suppose there's no harm in telling you. As long as you promise to keep this to yourself."

Mattie nodded.

"What if this is evidence of the cause of the fire?"

Mattie frowned. "Really? But that would mean—"

"Arson. Yes. And it might not be, and I know that, but I also think the sheriff needs every single little speck of information that is available. Your father and I didn't tell you, but the insurance company is holding any payout until the case is closed or resolved in some way. Which means we need to nudge Sheriff Sands if possible."

"This isn't . . . I don't know . . . interfering, is it?"

"I don't think so. It's just making sure the sheriff knows what we know. And you'll answer any of his questions if he wants to follow up, won't you?"

"Yes, of course, if it helps, but . . . wow. Do you really

think someone could have set that fire on purpose? Why would someone do such a thing?"

"I don't know, Matilda." Her mother sighed. "You're old enough to know by now. There are people in the world who are so hurt or angry or neglected that they lash out at the world around them. It could have been anyone for any reason, really."

"Or it could have been an accident."

"That's true. And that's what the sheriff is trying to figure out."

She made a fist, clutching the button so tightly that Mattie wondered if the edge of it was cutting into the flesh of her palm.

"I'm going to go see the sheriff right now. Before I lose this." She stood and walked to the door of the room. "Are you all right?"

"Yes, Mama, I'm fine . . . Are you?"

"I will be. It makes me feel better to be able to do something about this. Thank you for this."

As Mattie watched, her mother left and closed the door behind her.

She closed up the cigar box and tied the ribbon again to hold it shut before tucking it back under her cot. Maybe the next thing she would put in there could be Duncan's train ticket from when he finally came out west from Philadelphia.

CHAPTER TWENTY-FIVE

It was yet another laundry day.

It seemed to Edith as though it was always laundry day. She had church on Sundays and the occasional social commitment like the fundraising committee meetings, but otherwise her days were remarkably the same and there always seemed to be laundry to do.

It was monotonous, truth be told, but that was one of the hazards of having so many guests in her boarding house. She did not have the time or energy to change the sheets for all of the beds at the same time; she did two or three each week, round and round on a never-ending rotation. It was a routine that had served her well for years, though she admitted to daydreaming about hiring someone else to do this all for her. She had heard only good things about the Meyer family that ran the laundry farther down on Main Street.

Maybe someday she could justify that cost. Not yet, though.

Today was the day she stripped the linen from her

own bed, Daisy's, and Bill's. If the latter left on time, which was in no way certain, she could get started immediately after breakfast. Once she'd confirmed Daisy had begun washing the breakfast dishes, Edith climbed the stairs to begin her day. Since her own bed was always last —in case she ran out of time—she left the clean linens in there before starting with Bill's room near the end of the hall.

Edith knocked gently, just double-checking that Bill was out. She'd seen him at breakfast, but she hadn't seen him leave the house. When she felt she'd given enough time to be sure he was not in his room, she let herself in.

As the door swung open, she froze.

There was something wrong here. She could sense it but could not immediately identify what it might be. Something ever so slightly off about the room.

This was her tenant's room. She had every intention of honoring his privacy. But if something was wrong, it was her duty to fix it.

Before entering, she sniffed. That was it. There was some smell in this room that she wasn't used to, a smell that didn't match anything else in her house. But she couldn't identify what it was, and without that she would not be able to track it down. Hoping against hope that she would not find some piece of rotting food tucked away in the back of the closet or under a pillow, Edith got to work stripping the sheets from Bill's bed.

She hummed to herself as she worked; tedious though the chore was, she had long ago become quite efficient at it. Her hands seemed to move on their own, while her mind was occupied elsewhere, planning the menu for the quilting circle that would be meeting in a little over a week. Daisy had a delicious lettuce salad that would be perfect this time of year, with all the summer vegetables at the peak of their season. Edith would have to remember to go to the Eatons' to see if they could spare enough fresh produce for all the ladies she was expecting. There was also the beef bones to get from the butcher, to make a stock that would go a long way to feeding this large group of women. That would be the ideal summer lunch, Edith thought. Hearty soup, fresh vegetable salad, and warm, crusty sourdough bread, sending her guests home full and happy without heating up the whole house with a roast or something similar.

As for dessert . . .

Edith hummed while she stuffed the pillow in a clean pillowcase and thought about dessert. Daisy had found a recipe for a summer berry trifle that she had been begging Edith to let her try. Perhaps that would be just the thing for her to suitably impress the women of Juniper Falls with her domestic prowess and taste. But then, trying a new recipe was always a risk. Could she afford for Daisy to make a practice trifle ahead of time?

It did sound delicious, though. Edith wondered if she could cut back somewhere else in the budget to make room for it.

Before she left the room with the soiled linen, Edith took one more look around the room. Just as she had with Silas and Jack, she wanted to be certain she wasn't leaving behind a dirty dish or something else that might attract insects and vermin. Nothing seemed out of place, though there was a messy pile of dirty laundry in the corner of the room, under the window.

Always more laundry indeed.

She shook her head at this man's slovenliness, and tentatively kicked through the dirty clothes just to be certain there wasn't anything underneath that would become a surprise later on. One of the shirts was missing a button right in the middle, but that was not Edith's responsibility. All her tenants used the Meyers' laundry down the street for their clothing, and Mrs. Meyer could sew on a new button for him.

Before nudging the pile back into place, Edith's eyes caught on something else.

The shirt that was missing the button was crumpled up, partially in a ball, so she almost missed noticing it. Upon closer reflection she realized that the cuff of the right sleeve was ever so slightly singed.

She was so surprised that she took an unconscious step back.

There were only so many reasons that a man might have burnt—and then hidden—his shirt. While most of those reasons were perfectly innocuous—accidents, clumsiness, not paying attention to where he tossed a worn shirt—Edith's mind went immediately to the injurious.

There had been a huge fire in Juniper Falls only a few weeks prior . . . a fire that everyone in town had heard about, and one whose cause they still did not know.

Edith could not remember where Captain Stuart had been that day.

It was long enough ago—and her days really did all seem very similar—that she didn't think anyone would blame her for the gap in her memory, but for her own peace of mind she wished beyond measure that she could remember.

She realized she had frozen in her shock at the sight of the singed shirt sleeve, and shook herself back to awareness.

It might be nothing—she knew that. It might be nothing, but she would never be able to live with herself if she treated it as though it were nothing. So much of the captain's erratic behavior came to mind, and Edith had to admit that if there were anyone in Juniper Falls that she could believe this of, it was him.

She wanted to take a deeper, more thorough look around the room, but she did not trust herself to remain nonchalant should he return while she was still in here. Edith very much wanted this to be someone else's concern.

She knew just what to do.

Gathering all the soiled bed linen in her arms, Edith hurried back downstairs into the kitchen and dropped it all in a pile on the floor. Daisy looked up at her in surprise from where she had been drying the dishes she'd just finished washing.

"Can you get the laundry started for me?"

"I— Yes, of course. Is everything all right?"

"Maybe . . . I'm not sure." She pulled off her apron and hung it on the hook by the door. "The truth is that I need to find Sheriff Sands. He can be the one to decide if this is a problem or not. I'll be back as soon as I can, but right now I can't—" Her heart began to pound as the reality of what she had learned sunk in. "Thank you, Daisy. I'm all flustered. Do I look all right? Hair in place and all?"

"You're welcome. You look perfect. Be careful. I'll

handle all of this, so just take your time." She looked at Edith with concern but didn't push for an explanation.

Her mind full of what she would say to the sheriff, how she would explain what she had seen, Edith hurried back through the house to her front door. When she pulled it open, the doorway was filled with a tall, wiry shape. She squeaked in alarm, stepping back from the figure, who had seemed just about to enter a moment earlier.

"Oh! Goodness . . . Captain Stuart. You startled me."

She prayed he could not hear the quaver in her voice, could not see her hands shaking. She almost missed completely what the man said, so preoccupied was she in realizing that, if she had stayed in his room for one minute longer, then perhaps . . .

"Excuse me," she said, stepping out of his way so he could enter the house.

As was his wont, the man simply frowned at her but didn't say anything more. She had an idea that if she had not stepped out of his way, he may have just barreled into her anyway. After glaring silently at his landlady, he headed upstairs.

As he started up the steps, Edith remembered something.

"Oh, and Captain! I've just changed your bed clothes. Just so you know, in case you notice anything amiss in your room. I was just in there briefly."

He grunted his reply—thanks? irritation?—and continued stomping up the stairs.

Edith blinked in surprise—how did that man always seem to be able to give the rudest possible reaction?—before continuing on her path. She closed the front door behind her and paused on her front porch to catch her breath. If she was going to have second thoughts, now was the time to stop herself. Before she said something she could not take back. Before she maligned a man's reputation and name.

But at that thought, Edith realized that the man in question already *had* a questionable reputation. And she wasn't about to do anything more than report a fact. It would be up to Sheriff Sands to do with that fact what he will.

With that thought to comfort her conscience, Edith stepped down the few stairs from the porch and began her walk down Main Street. She nodded politely to friends she saw along the way, but she did not allow herself time to stop. If she did not do this now, she was sure she would be talking herself out of it later and she had no time for dilly-dallying.

Soon, Edith stood in the doorway of the office, wringing her hands.

"Sheriff. You asked me to come see you if I thought of anything else or found anything that might provide more information about the fire at the inn?"

He took one long look at her, before nodding to one of the chairs that sat in front of his desk. "Have a seat, Mrs. Bennett. Tell me what you know."

CHAPTER TWENTY-SIX

"So, then my mother took this little button all the way to the sheriff's office. Can you imagine?" Mattie concluded. "When she came back she didn't say anything, and I haven't asked. I suppose if anything is to come of it we'll know eventually. Mrs. Bennett seems distracted too. I wonder what all is going on . . ."

Lillian and Mattie had met at the Sunshine Cafe just before lunch to go over their plans for the Christmas concert before Mr. Nolan came to meet them for whatever help the newspaper would be able to provide. They hadn't seen each other in a few days, and Lillian was fascinated to hear what was going on behind closed doors at the boarding house.

She herself had been sticking close to home, helping Mary Ann as much as she could and being home waiting for Ned whenever he returned from the store at the end of the day. There was a nagging feeling in the back of her mind that this chapter of her life would be coming to an end soon. Mary Ann would leave them eventually. They would likely have children soon after. All this freedom that Lillian had enjoyed in the summers would soon be a memory, and she was torn between taking advantage of what might be the last time she could take advantage of such liberties and keeping the peace with her husband.

This morning, for example, she had neglected to mention to him this meeting with Mattie and Mr. Nolan. Lillian had told herself that Ned was in a hurry, that if he was interested in how she was going to spend her day then he would have asked. But the truth was she had spent all morning he was home hoping the subject would not come up.

This felt like the last thing that would be hers alone, and Lillian wanted to protect it.

"Goodness," she said, when Mattie had finished telling her about the button. "We've only lived in Juniper Falls for a little over a year. In the spring there was something about the sheriff at the time trying to help a man buy up a bunch of over-leveraged property, but I don't know all the details about that. Otherwise, everyone here seems so . . . trustworthy."

"I guess you never can tell."

"I guess not. And the town is growing pretty quickly, it seems, so maybe some uncouth person blew in and left again or . . . I don't know."

"This new sheriff, though—Sands? He's a good one, isn't he?"

"I think so. I don't know him any better than I know Mr. Sharp, though."

"Right. So, Mr. Nolan's meeting us today," Mattie said, getting back to the subject at hand. "You remember everything that was decided at the meeting yesterday? I should have written something down. I swear, the more I try to focus the more scattered I feel."

"I remember," Lillian assured her. "Benefit of being a teacher, I suppose. I always feel like I have to be prepared to speak with authority on something."

Mattie laughed. "You saying that just made me realize I always feel ready to speak, whether I feel prepared or have authority or not. I should try to rein in that impulse, I'm sure."

"It's part of your charm," Lillian assured her.

The front door of the cafe opened, and the women looked up to see Jeffrey Nolan enter, look around quickly, and then, spotting them, smile and head to their table. Mrs. Jenkins was right behind him, taking his order for coffee and pie before he had even gotten settled in.

Lillian and Mattie had sat on one side of the booth when they arrived at the cafe, allowing Mr. Nolan to slide into the other. After pleasantries, waiting for his order, and their own coffee refilled, he focused on the business they had come for, with his notepad on the table next to his plate of pie and a pencil in hand.

"All right, ladies. Thank you for meeting me. I thought I'd take the chance to ask you some questions and get an idea of the event before we make any sort of definite plan. You said it's a Christmas concert?"

"That's right," Lillian said. "There's a few months between here and there, so we were hoping you would have space in the paper for at least a couple different articles or advertisements."

"As much space as you can spare," Mattie said,

excited. "We want to set records with the attendance of this concert."

He nodded while rapidly taking notes. "Mm-hmm. We'll see what we can do. And tell me again what we are raising funds for."

"The schoolhouse. It needs a new coat of whitewash and a row of juniper trees between the yard and the road to protect the children," Lillian said.

"You're one of the teachers, are you not, Mrs. Frye?"

"I am, yes. For the last year."

He fixed an intent gaze on her before continuing. "It is unusual for a married woman to teach, isn't it?"

"Yes," she replied, adding, perhaps a bit too quickly, "but I love my work, and my husband was supportive."

She'd tried not to put too much emphasis on the past-tense word, tried to avoid adding *for now* to the end of her sentence. No one needed to know what she and Ned discussed in their own home.

"So then, of course, you will personally benefit from the fundraiser being successful."

Lillian frowned at what she thought was a challenge from the reporter. "Um . . . I suppose. But any family with school-age students would also benefit. And if those educated students stay in or near Juniper Falls in the years to come, the whole town will benefit. Wasn't it Horace Mann who said that universal education was essential to our democracy?"

"Was it?" he asked absently as he continued to write. "I'll have to look that up."

Lillian looked at Mattie. Why did she feel as though she were being interrogated?

"And who else is on the fundraising committee?"

"Mrs. Langdon," Mattie said promptly, smartly leading with their most prominent member. "Mrs. Trill, Miss Wright, Mrs. Jarrett . . . who else? Oh! My mother, who is the new owner of the inn. Once it gets rebuilt."

"Other ladies too. We can get you a full list if that's necessary," Lillian added.

"All right." He finished scribbling a sentence before looking up at them expectantly. "What else? Give me any detail you can think of."

The two women exchanged a look. Mattie gestured for Lillian to continue.

"It will be on December twenty-third, and though it is not yet officially decided, the current intention is to rent out the Lantern Theater. I don't know how many seats it holds, but we can find out."

"Good." He nodded as he jotted down his notes. "Smart. Implying a scarcity of opportunity will make it more likely to sell out."

"Really?" Lillian asked. She wondered if Ned had ever tried making known limited quantities in his stock, to encourage more people to buy. She shook her head. Now was not the time to question her husband's business instincts.

"And who will be performing?"

"The students, for the most part. The older ones, primarily, but Mrs. Langdon will probably want to put together a recitation for the younger students, like her daughter. We might see if Mabel Price will sing? She has a beautiful voice and doesn't get nearly enough attention for it. Although, really, anyone who wants to donate their time and talent to the cause would be welcome. Someone mentioned trying to get a professional singer from Cheyenne, but that seems unlikely. You would want to talk to Mrs. Armstrong on the entertainment subcommittee, though. I don't know what they have decided thus far."

"Do you know what tickets will cost?"

The two women looked at each other again.

"I . . . don't know," Mattie said. "I think maybe Mrs. Langdon mentioned it, but the conversation moved to some other detail before anything was decided."

"That's right. Mrs. Langdon. Maybe I should be talking to her?"

Lillian nodded. "She's the head of the entire committee, and I think she's on the subcommittee for the location. But, knowing her, she might just plan on having a foot in each of the subcommittees. I'm surprised she hasn't asked us specifically about our plan so she can be part of it."

"She is a remarkable woman. Quite the presence in this town, don't you think?"

"I'm too new to town to say for certain," Mattie said. "But she has been very welcoming."

"I agree." He finally sat up straight and then leaned back in his seat, taking a break from his notes. "When I first moved here she invited me over for Sunday dinner once a month for several months in a row. I think until some other orphan or lonely person moved to town. I will never not be grateful for the way she tried to help me feel at home."

He took a bite of his pie, now much cooled from when Mrs. Jenkins had first served it.

"You know," he continued as he made quick work of the pie slice, "I wonder if she would be interested in being interviewed for a full profile about the concert. Her influence could go a long way toward getting people's attention and investment in the project."

Mattie made an indistinct noise in her throat, and Lillian glanced over to see that her friend had gone pale. She cleared her throat, which turned into a cough, and Lillian finally answered Mr. Nolan.

"Well, again, knowing Mrs. Langdon, she would probably be happy to help however you need. Did you want us to ask her?"

"I don't know." He pulled some cash out of his wallet and dropped it on the table. "Let me think about it first. I need to check with Sharp, anyway, about how much space we have to spare. You know there's rumors that that fire was arson, so we might have an arrest or trial to cover too."

"Wait—Mr. Nolan!" Mattie lunged forward, grabbing the man's forearm before he could get up. "Did you say *arson*? Are you sure?"

He shrugged. "Just a rumor. Sharp told me. I don't even know where it started. Maybe we spend column inches investigating it. Maybe nothing happens. My point is that we chase breaking news, so this little school concert is not necessarily going to be a priority. I just wanted you ladies to understand that I'll do the best I can, but I can't make any promises."

Seeing that Mattie was too stunned to answer, Lillian responded. "We understand. Thank you, Mr. Nolan, and please do let us know how else we can help."

He nodded, scooping up his notebook and heading out the door.

When Lillian looked at her friend again, the other woman seemed dazed.

"Did you hear that?" she asked in a whisper.

"Arson," Mattie said. "Why would someone want to do that to my family?"

Lillian had no answer. She squeezed her friend's hand sympathetically, glad she was safe in the boarding house now and thankful the McBrides had not been in the hotel when someone set fire to it.

CHAPTER TWENTY-SEVEN

Charlotte came down the stairs at the boarding house just in time to see Mrs. Bennett spill a cup of tea across the dining room table, and then be completely flustered by both that and the fact that it had been witnessed.

"Oh! Let me help you," she said, rushing to her landlady's side. Scooping up a rag that had been sitting on the sideboard, Charlotte moved swiftly to stop the spread of tea from dripping off the side of the table.

"I am just all thumbs today," Mrs. Bennett muttered, going to the kitchen to get more rags.

Something was going on. A couple days earlier, Charlotte had passed the sheriff as he left the boarding house, though he had only acknowledged her and continued on his way. There had been no further update about any of the information around the inn, the fire, or the investigation. The rest of the time, their landlady had seemed occupied, as though she always had one ear cocked toward the front door of the boarding house.

More than once Charlotte had to repeat her question to the woman.

But then, Charlotte herself had been distracted as well. After she had taken the button to the sheriff, he had heard everything she had to say, accepted the item, and filed it away carefully in an envelope meant to protect evidence. But then that had been it. He had sent her home again, being very tight-lipped about how or where the investigation went after that. She had no idea if she'd been helpful or a hindrance.

Whatever happened with the sheriff, Charlotte was looking forward to their inn construction being finished, to putting this period of stress and uncertainty behind them. Mr. Chandler had been working on the property for a few weeks now, and the couple of times she had gone by to see the progress had been at least apparent. He refrained from giving the McBrides any definite timeline, however.

So in the meantime, Charlotte just tried to stay on top of all the things that needed tending to—the moving schedules and changing budget and uncertainty in every direction.

After helping Mrs. Bennett clean up a little, she had settled onto the settee in the parlor with her needlepoint when her husband entered. It was midafternoon, and she had not seen Henry since just after breakfast.

"Hello, darling," he said. "I was looking for you."

"Why? Is everything all right?"

"Oh, fine. Just wanted to talk to you. But . . ." He looked around. "Somewhere more private, maybe. I need to go over a few things with you. Can you meet me up in our room?"

Charlotte nodded, suppressing a sigh; with as much as the McBrides had going on, it seemed like there was always some news, always some reason they needed to talk over next steps. She gathered her things again and climbed the stairs ahead of him.

When Henry entered their room a few minutes later, he closed the door quietly behind him. Despite his wearing a hat every day, Charlotte noticed the smallest hint of freckles scattered across his nose and cheeks. He had been in the sun far more in the last few weeks than in the previous years they had been in Philadelphia. She was hopeful that her husband would find health and renewed vitality after coming west, and it seemed to be occurring.

"All right. Two things." Henry took a deep breath and sat down on the edge of the bed next to her. Before he continued, he looked around at their confined space. "I will be so grateful when we can move into the hotel. Even just having a chair in here would make a difference, but there's simply no space, is there?"

"What were the two things, Henry?" Charlotte knew she would not be able to focus on anything until she heard what he had come to tell her. "Should I be worried?"

"Yes. Sorry. I haven't heard anything specific, but last night, when Chandler and I were at the saloon, we couldn't help overhearing the men at the next table. Now, it's possible they were all talk—no telling how much they'd already had to drink. But they were talking about how there's an arsonist in Juniper Falls."

Charlotte gasped. "No! What did the sheriff say?"

"Nothing. I don't know. Like I say, it seems to be just

a rumor. I don't know how seriously to take it, or how much the sheriff is considering it. And, really, the whole story could have originated anywhere, but maybe people saw you visiting the sheriff's office and jumped to some conclusions? I don't know. I just want you to be careful, please. We can't risk the perpetrator getting wind and leaving town. Our best hope for any of this is that the investigation is seen through to the end."

"Of course. I didn't even tell Matilda why I wanted the button she'd found. Wherever this rumor is coming from, it's not me."

"I know, darling." He took her hand in his. "The other thing is . . . I got a telegram today."

"Did you? From who?"

"From the insurance company."

Charlotte had been fiddling with her ring, but stopped and looked at him sharply. The tone of his voice was ominous, and she wasn't sure she could handle any more bad news.

"A telegram. Not a letter? What did it say?"

"That Sheriff Sands is pursuing evidence that suggests the fire that burned down the General Sherman Inn was the work of an arsonist." He sighed. "So however the rumor started, it's unfortunately based in fact. But . . . it does mean that the next part of the insurance payout we were hoping for is going to be delayed."

"Oh! No . . . oh, no, Henry. Who— Why— What does that mean? Who would do such a thing? What do we need to do?"

"Calm down, my darling. There's nothing we *can* do right now except wait."

"You know perfectly well that is the absolute worst

thing you could ask me to do," she said, half-laughing. "I can't sit still. I'd rather walk all the way back to New York to speak to someone there."

He smirked. "At least take some money with you to get on a train back to me."

"Very funny, Henry McBride. Tell me everything."

"Not much more to tell. The sheriff is still investigating, but somehow the story is leaking across town. We can either stay out of the sheriff's way or . . . I don't know. Bullock and I have looked over the policy paperwork now three times. As far as I can tell, there's no restriction on the money if it does turn out to be arson from some outside person. The hiccup, though, is that as long as the investigation is still in progress, the claim remains still in progress. So what we need to do is have the sheriff close the case entirely *or* make an arrest."

"Oh, goodness. You've talked to Sheriff Sands, haven't you? That man has integrity. He's not going to do either one of those options without good reason."

"Exactly. Which means we're back to my initial assessment. We wait."

She groaned and lay back on the bed. The money was simply draining from their bank account. She'd been afraid that they would have to pause the construction if they couldn't raise the funds to pay for the workers and materials. But if they halted the construction, it would be just that much longer before it was done and they could welcome guests. And now there was this news, this very clear delay in having everything settled.

"I feel . . . hopeless. Useless. I hate that there's nothing I can do."

"I know, my love. I wish I had better news for you."

He took her hand again, gently, holding it, silently reassuring her of his presence and support.

"And how close are we to having the inn finished?" she asked, still lying back on the bed with her eyes closed.

Henry sighed. "Chandler says another few weeks. So, maybe double that, assuming that we have the money we need to pay for all the steps necessary. Did you place the order for the furniture?"

"No, I—" She sat up suddenly and turned to Henry, still clutching his hand. "I looked at the catalog, but the prices all seem . . . Oh, Henry, I don't know how we're going to be able to furnish the entire place. But I also know that we have to place the order last week in order to get whatever furniture we need here when the place is ready to open."

"We can't have an empty hotel," her husband said.

"What are we going to do?"

He took a deep breath. "I don't know. There's nothing we *can* do, other than what we're already doing. Maybe the solution will find us."

He hung his head, and Charlotte noticed more gray flecks in the hair above his ears. He was working so hard for them, and she felt badly that she couldn't take more off of his plate. Maybe she'd go back to the general store to look over the catalog again. Surely there must be some way to make this all work.

"Do you wish we had stayed in Philadelphia?" she asked quietly.

He looked up at her again and smiled faintly. "Sometimes. At least there I knew what to expect all the time. No surprises."

"No adventure, though," she added.

"No adventure," he agreed.

"Although right now I feel as though we've had more than enough adventure."

"It will all get sorted. Eventually."

"Eventually," she echoed with a sigh.

Charlotte rested her head on her husband's shoulder and the pair sat quietly together, each with their own thoughts. She had always been so eager to work, so perfectly capable of getting whatever needed to get done accomplished, and now, when it seemed like there was so much out of her control, she was at a loss.

CHAPTER TWENTY-EIGHT

Mattie frowned. It had been a few days, but she could not stop thinking about the efforts she and Lillian had made to promote the upcoming Christmas concert. The meeting with Mr. Nolan, the reporter from the *Juniper Falls Gazette*, had been going smoothly until Mrs. Langdon's name had been mentioned. Though Mattie knew, objectively, that of course Mrs. Langdon was a wonderful option, of course the pastor's wife would be a more impactful interview subject than newcomer Mattie McBride would be, she hated to admit that she had imagined herself the center of the campaign.

After breakfast, Mattie had gone out onto the front porch of the boarding house. It faced west, almost straight down Main Street, so she was able to sit and watch folks running their errands, going to work, greeting friends and neighbors, just from where she sat. The weather was still cool, though Mrs. Bennett had told them to expect another couple weeks of hot weather before autumn truly arrived.

Mattie watched a young couple holding hands as they walked toward the farther end of the street, and tried not to think about Duncan. She missed him dreadfully, and was afraid that if too much time passed, he wouldn't come out to the territories that year. Snow and ice could delay trains, and he was far too practical to risk it. Though she had no idea how his father's health was, could she really wait another six or eight months to see him?

The front door of the boarding house opened and her mother came out.

"There you are," she said. "Will you be joining us for the quilting circle today?"

"That's today?" Mattie said. "Would you be very put out if I didn't?"

"No, dear. I don't blame you. It will be a lot of older women who you don't know, and let's be honest . . ." She smiled at her daughter indulgently. "You never pay attention to your sewing when it's a social event. If you stayed I would ask you to help Mrs. Bennett, anyway. You should enjoy your day. Whatever you had planned. But you might want to go up to our room if you don't want to get roped in."

Mattie stood, smoothing down her skirt. "Then I shall be off," she said with a grin. "Maybe take a walk or . . . I don't know. But it's too nice of a day to be cooped up inside sewing. I don't envy you at all."

"I need to make friends somehow," her mother said. "I'm not like you, darling. But you go have fun."

She kissed her mother's cheek, walked down the porch steps, and was soon on Main Street. There was a tiny bit of money in her pocket, but she wasn't hungry, she didn't need anything, and, more than finding somewhere to shop, Mattie just wanted to get to know Juniper Falls. She would take a walk, take her time. Not just any walk, but one where she ventured away from Main Street. So far, visiting the general store, the newspaper, the church, and the cafe, she hadn't gone any farther than the main thoroughfare that ran straight through town. With the exception of the Fryes' home, Mattie realized she hadn't really seen much of the town at all.

She told herself that she needed to know where to find the doctor, where to find the sheriff, where to direct guests who eventually came to stay at the inn. Some kind of concierge service would be necessary to help their inn stand out and give visitors a reason to stay. That could be Mattie's responsibility.

Today, she would walk. All through the town, taking it all in and learning the layout.

Mrs. Jarrett, the barber's wife who Mattie recognized from the fundraising meeting, waved to her from across the street. Mattie could feel herself beaming.

She walked a couple blocks along Main, then turned left at Market Street, just past the general store and half a block before reaching her family's inn. There were still a couple streets' worth of businesses before the residential neighborhoods and outlying farmland. The streets were wide enough for a stagecoach to pass by going in both directions. She was no city planner, but it seemed to her as though the town was well laid out to accommodate growth in population for decades to come.

She stopped outside the seamstress's shop, one block south of Main Street, arrested by the sight of a gorgeous dress on display in the front window. It was a rich forest green, with a high collar trimmed with just the barest hint of delicate lace. The long sleeves ended in a slight bell, which, when worn, would gently fall back to reveal the wearer's slender wrists. The skirt was full, with layers concentrated in the back, creating a desirable silhouette without being too overwhelming.

Suddenly, Mattie could picture herself wearing this dress to meet Duncan at the train. To host a dinner with their loved ones in their home. To stand in front of Pastor Langdon and be married to this wonderful man whom she had cared about for so long.

She grinned; a new bride deserved a new dress.

Mattie, somehow, could only picture herself in this gown in Juniper Falls, but she assumed that was because it had been so long since she had been in Philadelphia. She'd had a favorite dressmaker in that city, and though they had only afforded the occasional investment to have a dress professionally fitted, she'd so loved having that service convenient. Mattie knew she'd never be as skilled as a professional and had always been grateful for the chance to have fine things.

Now, living on the frontier, it would be the same. She and her mother would do most of their sewing, and she would need to save her pin money for the small luxury of paying someone better than her at it if she wanted nice dresses.

It was no matter if there was nowhere fancy where she could be expected to wear a nice dress. To Mattie it was worth it. She adored having nice things. The way she felt in a well-made gown was just as much of a benefit as the way she looked in it. Her entire mood was exhilarated just from a bit of luxe fabric.

She was pulled out of her reverie by the sound of a bell dinging over a shop door. Jack Kinsey exited the barbershop that sat a block north of her. He'd just gotten a trim; Mattie noticed a thin patch of pale skin on his neck that had until recently been covered by his shaggy, sandy-colored hair. He grinned at her, the single dimple in his left cheek flashing.

"Hey, there, Miss McBride. You all right?"

She looked up at him. "Yes. Why?"

"It's just that . . . I'm not sure you've moved from that window for at least ten minutes or so. I saw you from inside." He indicated to the barbershop that, likewise, had a big glass front window. "I know men like to joke about how much their wives shop, but it seems to me you must have seen all there is to see in that window. Do you feel faint?"

She laughed. "No. Oh, no, I'm sorry, I was just . . . I was miles away. Thinking about . . . well. A lot of things."

"That dress?" He winked at her.

"Of course this dress. *Look* at it." She gestured excitedly to the window, where the dress form stood stately and pristine, the skirt of the gown draped perfectly. "The lace, and the tiny pearl buttons, and the color . . ." She groaned. "I love it so much."

"Are you gonna buy it?"

"Not yet. But maybe. Actually, I was just taking a walk around Juniper Falls. Since I may be here for a while, I thought it would be a good idea if I get to know the geography a bit more. I imagine once we open the inn and have guests, there will be all kinds of questions I'll be expected to answer."

"You say that like you expect to leave sometime," he said with a slight frown.

"Oh, yes." She looked out toward the center of the street, where a young boy was struggling under the weight of a bushel of apples. She used the distraction as a reason to not have to look at Jack directly when she said this. "My beau will come out here to marry me, sometime. When he can get away for long enough. And then we'll go back to Philadelphia to start our life."

"You're not living your life here?"

She looked at him, but realized when she saw his grin that he'd been teasing her.

"Different kind of life, I guess," she said finally. "I think that's why I am just standing here, drinking in the sights of this gown, or that man tightening his saddle straps, or that boy"—she pointed—"who I feel certain is going to drop those apples any minute. You know, my family hasn't even owned a horse before. There wasn't enough need when we lived in Philadelphia. Everything we wanted we could walk to."

"Never?" Jack took a full step back from her in his surprise. "Why, horses are . . . irreplaceable! They're my whole life. Walking is fine and all, but not riding horses? You're missing out."

"I've ridden in a stagecoach and a hansom cab. Does that not count?"

He shook his head. "A horse can be your friend, and sitting in the back while someone else manages the reins is nothing at all. I feel sorry for you."

She laughed, before she realized he wasn't entirely kidding.

"Come on," he said, taking another step down the boardwalk. "Let me show you. You never know—you may end up getting a horse one day. This way, at least, I can show you the basics of what you might need to pay attention to."

"I . . . I'm not sure."

"Oh, of course. If you have something else you needed to do today, please don't let me stop you. I meant no disrespect."

"It's not that . . ."

In fact, Mattie could not say *why* she was hesitating. Perhaps it was some unknown fear of the large animals. Perhaps it was not wanting to take up this man's time. Or, perhaps, she sensed a latent connection to Jack Kinsey, and the idea of uncovering it, of growing closer to this man who was not her sweetheart, worried her.

But then, Duncan was not here, and neither had he ever been the jealous type. Mattie told herself that whatever she could learn from Jack would be useful when Duncan did finally arrive. In fact, she already started to compose the letter to him in her head, finding some funny way to describe her awkward first steps or the animal's interest in her.

"You sure I won't be in your way?" she asked Jack. "This is your occupation. I could not forgive myself if I took up your day or got you in trouble."

"Part of my job is making sure that folks have everything that they need to best utilize these animals. We'll call it that. Training, or something. Come with me to the livery, and we'll get you in a saddle in no time."

With a hopeful glance back at the gorgeous green dress, Mattie followed Jack to the livery for her first real taste of what it meant to live on the wild frontier.

CHAPTER TWENTY-NINE

The day had arrived when Edith's quilting circle was scheduled to come sew at her boarding house. Usually there were always two or three of the women who bowed out, citing family illness or unexpected responsibilities. This month, however, seemed to be an exception. With the mystery of the inn's fire, and the new owners being part of her household, it seemed as though curiosity won out over any other responsibilities. Every single one of the thirteen women would be in her parlor in just over an hour, and she had no idea where she would put them all. Luckily, Daisy could just add more water and rice to the soup to help stretch the food for all the expected guests.

Mrs. McBride had gone out to the porch to talk to her daughter, but she soon returned and found Edith in the kitchen to offer her help.

"All right, Mrs. Bennett," she said. "Put me to work. What can I do?"

"I'm not sure there's much left to do. We did all the

deep cleaning yesterday. The food is all in process . . . I feel like I'm forgetting something, but I can't put my finger on it . . . Ah, well. It will hit me eventually."

"How long do we have before your guests arrive?"

"*Our* guests," Edith corrected. She looked at the clock. "Forty-five minutes. You're still on schedule, Daisy?"

"Yes, ma'am. The broth simmered overnight, and I just finished straining out the bones and things. I'll add the rice and vegetables for the soup next."

Edith shook her head. "I don't know why I didn't expect this many people to come. I should have known, with new folks in town they would want to meet."

Not to mention the rumors of an arsonist to gossip about, she thought but did not say.

"Where are we going to put them all?" she continued.

"What if we sit out on the porch?" Mrs. McBride suggested. "It may get a little warm in the afternoon, but until then it's an absolutely beautiful day."

"Oh, yes!" Daisy agreed. "When I was sitting on the porch last night, the scent of clover and lavender wafted over from the O'Briens' yard, and it was just *heavenly*."

"All right, yes, that's a good idea. And if any of the ladies need a break for any reason, they can come inside. Let's maybe move the dining room chairs out there. There's an extra chair in my bedroom too. It's too bad we didn't think about this sooner, before the boys went off to their jobs."

"We can handle it," Daisy said brightly. "I have a few minutes yet before I have to worry about the next part of this meal. I can help."

Mrs. McBride followed Daisy into the dining room, while Edith took a look around her kitchen. Daisy had it all in hand, as far as she could tell. Mrs. McBride would be a wonderful hostess, she thought, as long as she let herself take over the role instead of waiting for Mrs. Langdon or one of the other women to approve her. And that left Edith free to keep track of everything else.

In less than an hour, all the chairs in the house had been brought out to the front porch, where the morning breeze made the summer day feel cooler. Edith had hunted down her extra scissors and found a small bucket the ladies could use for any fabric and thread scraps. She checked and double-checked that Daisy had the meal in hand.

And then, a little earlier than Edith had hoped, the first knock sounded at the front door. Once two of the women—Mrs. Bullock and Mrs. Armstrong—had arrived, the rest of the visitors found seats on the porch as they came up the steps. Edith had stayed out front to greet her guests alongside Mrs. McBride, but soon enough the ladies had all gotten started on their project, cutting and stitching together the small squares of fabric. The rest of the day, Edith felt as though she was all over the place. She wasn't sure she had managed to sit down once after that first knock on the door.

She was taking another pitcher of lemonade out to her guests when she overheard the women diving into the latest piece of town gossip.

"I can't believe there's an *arsonist* in Juniper Falls," one of the ladies said. "This is not that sort of place, Mrs. McBride, I assure you."

"It's such a shame what happened," another lady said.

"A shame," someone else echoed.

Edith paused just inside the front door to listen before going out. She couldn't be certain, but the voices sounded like Mrs. Langdon, Mrs. Meyer, and Mrs. Bullock. She knew that many of her friends had seen her visiting the sheriff's office the previous week, and she was afraid that they may not speak plainly if she were part of the conversation.

"Oh, thank you," Mrs. McBride said. "Other than this one very unfortunate obstacle, I can assure you that this town has been safe and welcoming. Mr. Bullock was just so kind and helpful when we were corresponding, and Mrs. Bennett was so quick to rescue us from the street. I almost feel badly that the sheriff has to deal with this."

"My dear, please don't think this is your fault," Mrs. Langdon said. "No one had any idea who you were before you arrived. I'm sure that whoever set that fire did not do it because of you."

"I know you're probably right, but I can't help but wonder . . . If someone local had purchased the inn instead, would it still be standing? If we had come out to the frontier before now, would it have been spared? These are some of the many questions that keep me awake at night."

"Sheriff Sands is doing more than he's letting on, I suspect," Mrs. Bullock added. "My husband let slip that he was interviewed just a few days ago. If I were you, I wouldn't worry at all and I'd trust it's all in hand."

"I just will be happy to put all of this behind us," Mrs. McBride said with a sigh. "It will be an interesting story to tell later, but right now, being in the middle of it is simply exhausting. This is not the fresh new chapter my husband and I had hoped for."

From just inside the front door, Edith heard the sound of one of the women standing. Afraid of getting caught eavesdropping, she quickly opened the door the rest of the way and stepped outside.

"Can I refresh anyone's lemonade?" she asked the group.

Mrs. McBride, who had been the one to stand, looked relieved to see Edith. "I was just coming in to see if there was any of that delicious lemonade left. Thank you so much."

"Have a seat again, dear. Daisy says the soup will be ready in another twenty minutes or so, if you ladies want to finish up on whatever you've got in your hands. We'll take a break for lunch."

"I don't think this will take much longer," Mrs. Thrush said, looking over the patchwork progress in her lap. "Might even get the top done before lunch if we hurry."

In the time Edith had been inside and running around, the ladies of the quilting circle had pieced together three large swaths of patchwork. They were using a simple nine-patch quilt block, sewed into rows. The next step would be to piece together the three wide rows, before binding it all. The quilt top would be given to Edith, as the host of this month's event, who could then bind it all together with batting and a backing and do what she wanted with it. Every month this group of ladies joined their labor together to create the simple but sturdy work of art that the month's host would get. Some kept the finished quilts, some gifted, and some donated. Edith had not yet decided what she would do with hers this month—the peach and green shades did match the wallpaper in the room the McBrides were staying in—but it was gorgeous.

"Once again, ladies, I am in awe of our collective skill," she said, after pouring Mrs. Trill a fresh glass of lemonade. "I'm so honored to get such a finely made quilt like this."

"I think I might just have to join your quilting circle permanently," Mrs. McBride said. "If you'll have me. The inn will need so many new quilts, let alone everything else. Even if I hosted every month for the next year, I don't know that it would be enough."

"I'd been wondering about that," Mrs. Trill said as she sipped her drink. "Rebuilding the interior is just part of reopening the inn. Are you ready for all of that? Is there anything we can help you with? Other than maybe another quilt," she finished with a smile.

Mrs. McBride sighed. "So many things . . . I really should have ordered furniture a week ago in order to give it enough time to arrive here from back East, but we just don't have it in the budget to furnish the entire inn, and to complicate things even further, the cost of shipping just a couple pieces instead of more is prohibitive."

"Have you talked to my husband?" Mrs. Trill asked.

"Oh, goodness," said Edith, as she sat on the porch railing. "I forgot all about that!"

Mrs. McBride looked from one woman to another, confused. "Your husband? No, I don't think so. Mr. Bullock might have, though. He gave my husband a whole list of people to talk to."

"Josiah Trill is a carpenter," Edith explained. "He made these chairs, for example."

"He's just one person," Mrs. Trill said to Mrs. McBride, "so if you need to furnish the entire inn at once, he's not your man, but I know he'd be happy to start with a couple pieces for you. Fill out the place little by little. Of course, it won't be quite the same as the factory-made furniture you could order. And I promise he won't be the least bit offended if you decide you want more of that uniformity. But it is an option."

"I love that idea! Both being able to furnish a handful of rooms at a time and being able to have unique pieces that can help the inn stand out. I would much prefer to support one of our neighbors than one of the big furniture magnates back in Boston. Thank you."

Edith thought Mrs. McBride looked far more relieved and at peace than she had maybe since they had first arrived in Juniper Falls. Mrs. Trill had offered precisely the right solution.

"I should have thought of this," Edith said. "I'm so sorry. If you'd like, I can walk you and Mr. McBride to Mr. Trill's shop this time tomorrow."

"That would be wonderful. Oh, I'm so excited!"

Mrs. McBride's eyes shone with the hope that had been eluding her for the last few weeks, and Edith was glad she'd been able to help.

CHAPTER THIRTY

"Is Mary Ann home?" Ned asked, coming down the hallway from their bedroom.

Lillian had been in their sitting room. She had a needlepoint project on her lap, but for the past twenty minutes she had been staring out the front window, her hands idle. The new school year was set to begin in just a couple weeks, and though she knew she would be ready, she couldn't help but want to think up ways that she could improve her lesson plans, strengthen her skills, and best provide a safe learning environment for the young people of the town.

The Juniper Falls Primary School had two rooms—one for ages six through nine, one for ages ten through twelve. Older students attended the Juniper Falls High School on the other side of the road. Lillian had been teaching the youngest children, after their last teacher, Mr. Phillips, headed farther west to California the previous year. With as quickly as the town was growing, it seemed likely that they would need a third teacher—and a third classroom—for the younger children in the next couple years. Lillian was torn between wanting to be part of that and wanting to start her own family.

But then, she knew, she'd already put off that day longer than Ned would have liked. It was an unfortunate truth that she could not do both, and Lillian realized that by getting married at all the decision had already been made.

She'd looked up when Ned entered the sitting room, but it took a long moment before his question was understood.

"Oh . . . no. She's not. Silas had to make a trip to Laramie and asked her to go with him, so I told her to take the day. She might not be home until supper. Which reminds me . . ." Lillian sat up straighter. "I'm going to have to decide what we're having for supper. Do you have any requests?"

"I'm glad she's not here," he said, ignoring her question. He crossed the room to sit next to her on the sofa. "There are some things I've wanted to say to you, and it's best if we have privacy."

Lillian glanced at the clock on the mantelpiece to her right. Ned had come home for lunch, but he hated to leave the store closed for longer than an hour. He would have to leave in the next thirty minutes.

"All right," she said warily. "Is it . . . Am I in trouble?"

"There's been this . . . trouble between us. A tension. I thought you and I had always been on the same team, but now there's this disagreement, and I can't help but feel as though you are not considering my viewpoint."

Lillian frowned, concerned. "I'm sorry. I—I always

try to consider you and what you want. What . . . what are you referring to specifically?"

"I don't want you teaching this year," he said, direct for the first time. "And I thought we had agreed that you would only teach until the children came."

"I— But—" Lillian had been expecting this argument to come to the surface soon, but she was nevertheless stunned by her husband's rigidity. "But, darling, we— The children have *not* come. I'm not sure why you're upset by my still teaching. We agreed that I would teach until we became parents, and that has not happened yet."

"But it did!" he insisted.

Lillian had never seen her placid, easy-going husband so upset.

"Ned . . ." she began softly.

"I know—all right? I *know* that it did not all work out the way we hoped, but you have to admit we were close. I was so excited to be a father, and then . . . when it ended . . . Lil . . ."

She watched him, surprised to see so much emotion from Ned for the first time. He had been supportive and sorrowful when they'd lost the baby earlier that spring, but never once seemed to blame her or try to minimize her own pain.

But in all of that she had not realized how much it had meant to him.

"Lil," he said again. He grabbed her hands, holding them tightly. "I want a wife who is happy to be home. A woman who takes pleasure in caring for our house and our family. You are . . . you're not that," he concluded, his voice turning bitter.

Lillian bit back the temptation to be sarcastic and biting. As though she had somehow tricked him into marrying her. As though at any point in all the time they had known each other she had hidden the fact that she enjoyed teaching and wasn't that skilled of a cook.

"Ned," she said finally, her voice low in the effort to keep it steady. "I am doing my best. For you, for the children, for the school, and Mary Ann, and what you're asking of me is . . ."

She shook her head and looked out the window again.

"You're right that we agreed I would stop teaching when the children came, but to ask me to stop before that time is . . . it's asking me to be someone I'm not. You've seen how I'm just so lost every summer, without something productive to do. Do you want me to be like that all the time? Do you want me to be unhappy?"

"I want you to be happy at home."

"But that's not— That's not who I *am*, my love. Please understand. I don't want to just wait at home until there is a child to fill my time," she responded, looking at him again. "I am a person in my own right, Ned, not just your wife. Please try to support me as such."

He scoffed. "What do you think I am doing all day, every day, at the store if not supporting you?"

She swallowed hard. "My heart," she said in a whisper. "Support my heart and my desires and my—my—my *person*. Let me be myself for just a while longer before I am someone's mother. I promise you—I've promised in the past and I'll do it again as many times as it takes until you believe me—I *promise* you that I will be the best mother and homemaker I know how to be. I'll even get Mary Ann to teach me some of your favorite recipes. But you can't ask me to give up teaching before it's time."

He stood.

"I can see I am not getting through to you," he said sadly. "Just, do me a favor, will you, and really think about what you are saying. Think about what it means for me to see my wife working and what our neighbors might think about it. And, honestly, Lillian—"

She flinched. He so rarely used her full name.

"Honestly, I need you to think about what it is doing to us every day you decide to put other people's children ahead of our own."

He exited toward the front door, grabbing his hat from the hook on the wall.

"Don't worry about supper for me tonight," he said. "I'll eat at the saloon once I close up the shop. You can have your lazy, child-free evening without having to worry about taking care of your husband. I won't get in your way."

Lillian's mouth hung open in shock as she watched him leave.

For a long moment she was numb, processing everything he had said to her, what she had said to him. Trying to find an angle of the conversation in which she had done wrong.

Lillian burst into tears.

What could she do?

She hated that she was so hurting Ned, but at the same time she knew she'd be miserable if she just stayed home all day before there were any actual children of her own to care for. Mary Ann didn't need her. Ned was at the store all day.

Could she make herself unhappy, just to keep the peace?

It was tempting, Lillian had to admit. She would always enjoy teaching, but her husband and her marriage was the rest of her life. It was worth fighting for, therefore—worth preserving.

But then, with only a couple of weeks before the new school year started, it would not be fair to the students, to their families, to the other teachers, for her to leave now.

Lillian put her needlepoint project back in the sewing basket kept for such things, and tucked it away under the side table next to the couch. With Ned back at the store for the afternoon, and Mary Ann gone most of the day, Lillian would have the house to herself for hours.

It would be a good chance for her to practice being a full-time homemaker, albeit one without children to occupy her. The least she could do was give it a try, if just so she could tell Ned she really did make an attempt.

She looked around the sitting room, wondering how Mary Ann would have spent her day had she been home. What chores needed to be done?

Lillian had no idea where to even start.

CHAPTER THIRTY-ONE

After all the ladies from the quilting circle left the boarding house, Charlotte made a polite excuse and headed up to her private room. It had a been a long morning in the sun, and she was ready for a break. It was still well before supper, but she was tired from her day of meeting new people and playing hostess. Once in her own room with the door closed, Charlotte slipped off her shoes, unbuttoned the top of her high collar, and lay down on the bed.

She was well out of practice of hosting of any kind; hopefully, when the inn was opened and she had more of a day-to-day routine, it wouldn't take so much out of her.

Or maybe, she thought, Matilda could take over part of running the inn. At least until Duncan came to whisk her away. She was so much better with people—with strangers—than Charlotte herself had ever been.

Though arriving in Juniper Falls to find that their investment had been destroyed was harrowing in its own right, Charlotte could look back at the intervening weeks and appreciate that she had not been thrown into a situation and whole new career that she was not yet ready for. At least this way, she had a chance to get to know the town, get to know her neighbors, and not feel rushed. It had also allowed her the chance to stay at this boarding house and make friends with not just Mrs. Bennett but also her quilting circle, the school fundraising committee, and so much more.

She had to admit, there would be a part of her that missed living here when the McBrides eventually moved into the finished hotel.

Charlotte stayed in her room the rest of the afternoon, lying back with a cloth over her eyes. Though she was unable to sleep while thinking over any number of things, having the quiet alone time was exactly what she needed. She had no idea where her daughter had gotten off to, but both Matilda and Henry would be back by supper at the latest. Charlotte allowed herself this quiet break.

She did not know how much time had passed when she heard the door open. Sitting up, and letting her eyes adjust to the light again, she saw that her husband had returned. He hung his hat on the hook by the door and crossed the room to examine himself in the mirror.

"Welcome back," she said.

"How was your day?" Henry asked as he loosened his tie.

"You wear a tie to hammer boards together?" his wife asked, watching him amusedly.

"Chandler doesn't let me anywhere near the hammers, to be honest," he said, chuckling. "More times than not I'm only there to answer questions from him and any of the other curious onlookers that walk by. Who would have thought that so many people would be interested in our little inn? So, really, dressing well helps keep eyes on me instead of interrupting the men actually working."

"How is it looking?"

"Oh, Charlotte." His eyes lit up as he came to sit next to her on the bed. "I never would have believed he would have been able to get so much done in so short of a time, but by adding a couple more men to the team it looks like they'll be done in just another couple weeks. There's still more we can do, of course—putting in a real marble mantlepiece in the lobby, or a more decorative staircase rail—but that all can wait. The basics will be done and there will be walls and doors and finished hotel rooms."

"I can't believe that! Why . . . that means— Will we have vacancy in time for the harvest festival? Mr. Quinn told Matilda that the town gets visitors from all over the county."

"I think we'll have the structure done, yes, but . . ." He looked at her cautiously. "But furniture? Wallpaper? Will you feel ready?"

"Oh, goodness, darling, that reminds me. Today, one of the ladies of the quilting circle mentioned that her husband is a carpenter and could possibly create some of the furniture pieces we need. Mrs. Bennett said she'd take me—or us, if you want—over tomorrow so we can meet Mr. Trill and see his work. I know that getting one piece at a time isn't ideal, but I think it's a good solution for the distance and the money and . . . all of it."

"A local carpenter? Why didn't we think of that?"

"I don't know." She laughed. "A result of all those years in a big city with everything we could want just within blocks, I suppose. I can't tell you how relieved I am, though. It feels like everything is falling into place."

"I'm glad, my love." He pulled her hand to his lips and kissed it.

"There's one other thing."

Charlotte had been thinking about this for days—weeks, perhaps—but had hesitated bringing it up to Henry before she was ready, as she wanted to be certain. Her afternoon alone with her thoughts, after being around so many of their kindhearted neighbors, had given her that.

"Anything."

She looked at him, sitting up a bit straighter before voicing her request.

"I think I'd like a fresh start."

"You don't think that completely rebuilding the interior of the inn is a fresh start?" her husband asked with a small smile. "I'm happy to show you the ledger showing how much we are paying for this 'fresh start.' "

"I'm being serious, Henry."

"All right, then. But why?"

"I know perfectly well what the ledger says. But I mean for more than just us. For the town. For Juniper Falls."

"I'm not sure I understand. Those people have always known the General Sherman Inn."

"They have, but it's that same inn that was destroyed. There are people, like Mrs. Bennett, who have lived here for ten years and who know this building as the General Sherman Inn and, furthermore, who know that said inn was burned down. There's a feeling of . . . instability. Of being unsafe. I want to get rid of all of that."

"What are you suggesting?"

"Let's change the name."

"Change the name?"

"Do you really want to be the proprietor of a place that calls to mind all that death and destruction? I know that General Sherman is a hero to many, but I'm not sure it hits the right welcoming note that we want."

Henry looked away from her, thoughtful. "I don't know . . . We'll have to start over completely, without any kind of reputation. Anyone in Cheyenne or Laramie or neighboring towns who has recommended the General Sherman Inn will have to learn the new name. We will have to do a whole outreach program just to let folks know."

"We probably need to do that anyway, since the news that it burned down has surely spread. And isn't it lucky," she said with a grin, "that our daughter has spent the last couple weeks getting to know one of the reporters at the *Juniper Falls Gazette* and learning all about what is necessary to try to promote something?"

He looked back to her, taking in her hopeful expression, her set jaw that indicated she had made up her mind. Over the nearly three decades they had been married, Henry had learned that Charlotte rarely expressed a definite opinion unless she was absolutely certain. She would not have brought it up otherwise.

He nodded, resolute.

"All right, you've convinced me. Do you have any ideas for what you'd like to name the inn?"

"I've been thinking about it. Something simple. Something classic. Something that makes people feel like this is a softer, more comfortable place than an inn named after a ruthless general. I want the place to feel cozy and warm and like a home away from home, not just a convenient bed and roof."

"Should we ask Mattie? She's always got some idea or another."

"Maybe, but I rather like the idea of it being something for just the two of us. This is our second act, isn't it? Yours and mine. We always knew the children would leave and start their own homes, and this is ours."

He nodded and squeezed her hand. "I'll think about it, then. And you think about how you would like to celebrate officially making the inn open for business. That day will be here sooner than we think."

"There are so many people we have to thank. Maybe it would be nice to have a party of some kind. All the strangers who have become friends. All the kind gestures and the help. This could have been a very different experience if it weren't for the generosity of all these people."

"Then it seems like a party is just the thing. Just a few more weeks, my love, and then we'll be finally embarking on the big adventure we'd always planned."

He stood up and checked his reflection as he buttoned his collar again.

"Now," he said, offering her his hand. "Let's go downstairs. I could smell coffee already when I walked in, and Daisy told me there is leftover summer berry trifle that 'has to' be eaten. Care to join me for a little snack before supper?"

Charlotte put her hand in his. "I've already had more trifle than is good for me, but I'll come with you."

"So, what you're saying is we should get the recipe from Daisy," he joked as they headed down the stairs.

CHAPTER THIRTY-TWO

By the end of August, the construction progress on the inn was surprisingly close to being done. Both of Mattie's parents had reminded her over and over that they should assume Mr. Chandler would take longer than he estimated. Just in case. So as to not be disappointed. The third floor was still mostly a shell of its former self, and the McBrides would be waiting to finish that part of construction, but as an institution open for business it was almost ready.

Once the cooler mornings of the last week of August dawned, Mattie found herself helping her mother choose the select pieces of furniture they would need right away, as well as planning the big opening ceremony later in the month. To begin with, the inn would have the dozen small rooms of the second floor open to guests. If they could attract that many. The family would sleep in a small addition made to the back of the inn, to be close to the front desk and available to guests.

It was all happening.

"I can't believe it's gone so quickly," Mattie told Lillian as the pair walked through the latter's neighborhood. Mattie had gone from Mr. Trill's furniture shop to the Fryes' so the two women could walk together to meet the reporter at the Sunshine Cafe for another interview about the school's fundraiser. "I had it in my mind that we would be at the boarding house until Christmas at least."

"I'm sure your family isn't the only one looking forward to having the inn completed. Situated as we are between Laramie and Cheyenne, Juniper Falls gets a surprising number of visitors. Maybe Mrs. Langdon, or the mayor or someone, put a little pressure on Mr. Chandler."

"Whatever the reason, I'm excited."

They reached another intersection, and Mattie looked around at the main street of Juniper Falls, just as busy around lunchtime as it was most days. The two women had to pause to let a wagon laden with bales of hay pass in front of them. Jack Kinsey was driving, and he grinned at Mattie as he passed. In her joy at seeing him, she reflected that she really should go back to the livery one of these days to get another lesson.

"Do you ever ride horses?" she asked Lillian.

Her friend looked surprised at the change in subject. "No, not really. Ned talked a lot about it when we first moved here, but there's really no reason we need to. We just hired the stagecoach to take us to the train station the couple times we've needed to get farther than the edge of town. Why?"

Mattie shrugged. "It seems interesting. I probably have no need to learn either, especially once I'm back in

Philadelphia, but I hate to turn down the opportunity while I have it."

"Maybe eventually I will," Lillian said. "But probably not for a while. I'll start school on Monday, and then . . ." She cleared her throat, pausing.

Mattie waited, giving her friend space to feel comfortable saying what she wanted to say.

"Ned won't want me to teach beyond this year, though," Lillian said finally. "So we'll see what happens then."

As her friend equivocated, Mattie could sense that Lillian was leaving a lot unsaid about the entire situation. She didn't want to pry, but she did wonder.

"Do you not have plans for once you're done teaching?"

"Oh . . . well, it will probably be time to start a family, I imagine," she said lightly. "Look at that."

She pointed, clearly choosing to change the subject abruptly, and Mattie let it drop as she followed where Lillian indicated to look at a little boy, maybe seven years old, successfully juggling three apples to the delight of his friends watching. It was a pure, heartwarming moment, though Mattie wasn't sure why specifically her friend had pointed it out.

"Oh, that's . . . adorable."

They had reached their destination, however, and Lillian opened the front door of the cafe for Mattie. Whatever the schoolteacher was going through, Mattie just hoped that her friend had someone to talk to about it. If not her, then maybe Mary Ann.

She didn't have much time to worry about it, however, once she saw what was waiting for them.

When they entered the Sunshine Cafe, Mattie was surprised to see the reporter, Mr. Nolan, not just already there and seated, but also already in conversation with someone. Her back was to the door, so it wasn't until Mattie and Lillian went over to the table that she realized it was Mrs. Langdon.

"Oh! Ladies, I wasn't sure you'd be here."

Mr. Nolan stood to welcome them, and there was a bit of awkward shuffling to make room for the two new women. Mattie was too stunned to say anything at first; it seemed very apparent that they had been neither expected nor wanted. That surprised her; when she thought back over their last conversation with Mr. Nolan, she thought for certain he had asked for more information about the upcoming event.

"Um . . . here. Sit. Please."

He waved for Mrs. Jenkins, and in a few moments all four were seated, with coffee on the way.

There was an awkward silence all around the table as each person waited for another to initiate the conversation. Mattie looked around at the politely confused faces seated at the table.

"Well," she said finally, "I'm glad you got started right away. We're so excited that the paper is covering our event. Hopefully together we can provide you all the information you need?"

"Yes, um . . ." Mr. Nolan began. "Mrs. Langdon here was just telling me about the interior of the Lantern Theater and how ideal of a location it is going to be for her upcoming concert."

Mattie frowned. "Oh, yes. I guess I didn't realize that decision had been set."

"Well, dear," the pastor's wife said, "you're not a member of the location subcommittee, of course. Though I suppose your mother might have told you?"

"Right, well . . ." Mattie looked at Lillian, who was watching the conversation with pursed lips. "I assumed that, as we were in charge of promoting the event, we would have been made aware of all pertinent details. Is that not correct? I mean, we approached Mr. Nolan specifically for that purpose. I was looking forward to being interviewed, really."

She smiled at the older woman, trying to cushion the irritation in her tone. Mattie felt bewildered by the entire situation, and well out of her depth in dealing with a person of such standing in her new community.

"Why, Miss McBride," Mrs. Langdon said, "it didn't even occur to me that you would be up for speaking on such a subject. Didn't you only just move to Juniper Falls a month or two ago?"

"Well . . . yes. But . . . I'm a fast learner, and—" She looked from Mrs. Langdon, with her politely blank expression, to Mr. Nolan, his of utter confusion. "I really thought I was just doing what was expected of us. We have been tasked with promoting the fundraising concert after all, have we not?"

"I very much appreciate everything you have done to get our little event in front of a man such as Mr. Nolan," the pastor's wife said. "And I'm sure Mrs. Frye is as well, given her position. But now it's time for someone more knowledgeable and well-known to the community to take over. Any promotion will be far better received by our neighbors if they see my name attached to the event."

"Instead of mine," Mattie said flatly, finishing what Mrs. Langdon seemed intent on leaving unsaid. "I see."

"I think I do have everything I need for now, Mrs. Langdon," the reporter said. "I appreciate all your time this morning, and I'll be sure to let you know if the editor has any additional follow-up questions."

The older woman looked to the younger and slid out of the cafe booth.

"It was my pleasure. We're grateful for your help."

Mattie held her tongue. She couldn't even look at Lillian; she was too embarrassed and a little bit insulted to have been brushed aside as she had been.

When the pastor's wife was through the door and out of earshot, she turned to Mr. Nolan with a falsely bright smile.

"What other questions do you have that we can help you with? Did you hear that my family's inn will be open soon? We'll be able to take visitors from all over the county who want to come support the school."

"That's nice." He was scribbling some final notes and didn't seem to be listening to Mattie at all. "Mrs. Langdon's interview will take up several inches of space in the paper, though. I'm not sure we'll be able to squeeze in your news."

Mattie took a deep breath, ready to retort, ready to point out that the inn reopening should be big news in its own right, ready to ask him why he had turned to the pastor's wife instead of herself when it came to the Christmas concert.

But she caught the look of disengagement on Lillian's face and decided she did not want to pick a fight. Especially as her parents could benefit from having a friend at the *Juniper Falls Gazette*.

"Thank you for meeting with us," she said finally.

Mr. Nolan looked up from his wallet, where he had been pulling out cash. Mattie and Lillian had not even had a chance to order anything, and the meal was already over.

"Thank you," he said simply. Tipping his hat to both women, he too slipped out of the booth and out the door of the cafe.

Mattie watched Mr. Nolan walk away and sighed. She turned to Lillian.

"Am I wrong here? I thought— Why have a subcommittee for this kind of thing if she is just going to step in and do it herself anyway? I'm so . . . I shouldn't be as hurt as I am, but I am frustrated."

Lillian offered a sympathetic smile. "I don't know. But . . . what can we do? It's the pastor's wife. She's possibly the most beloved person in the entire town. *And* you have to admit she knows more about what is going on with the concert plans than we do."

"I know, I know. You're right, and I'm being . . . self-centered. I am trying to help and put down roots in this town, but . . ." She sighed. "Maybe I just wanted the excitement of seeing my name in the paper. How often is that going to happen?"

"Maybe when the inn reopens?"

"Maybe."

The two women decided not to stay at the cafe. Lillian wanted to get home to dig out her lesson plans before school started the following week, and Mattie had told her mother she'd help pick out wallpaper that afternoon. They said their goodbyes and went their separate ways, but Mattie couldn't quite shake her discontentment.

Mattie sighed. She made a detour to the post office before returning back to the boarding house. Maybe there would be a letter from Duncan waiting for her. That would cheer her up. He would be coming to take her away from Juniper Falls soon enough; any disappointments or clashes she had here would soon be in the past.

CHAPTER THIRTY-THREE

"I'll get the door," Edith told Daisy. She wiped her hands on her apron before untying it. "I wonder who it could be?"

"Maybe it's someone who wants to let the Watkinses' old room," suggested Daisy.

"Wouldn't that be a relief!"

The two women had been in the kitchen, washing the fresh vegetables that would be roasted with supper that night, when they heard a firm knock on the front door of the boarding house. As far as they knew, the two McBride women were in the parlor looking at wallpaper samples, but all the other tenants were out for the day. They were not expecting visitors or deliveries; Edith could not guess who might be knocking in the midafternoon.

The women looked up when Edith walked through the parlor, but they let her be the one to answer the door.

She was shocked to see Sheriff Sands standing on her front porch.

"I—well, this is a surprise. Is everything all right, Sheriff?"

"Mrs. Bennett." He took off his hat and fixed her with a somber expression. "Ma'am, I am so sorry about this."

"What is it?"

She looked over his shoulder to see that Deputy Inglis had joined him, standing a step back.

"We are here to arrest one of your tenants."

Edith gasped. Though she had reason to suspect one of the men under her roof had been up to no good, she had not truly allowed herself a chance to consider this possibility.

"I'm afraid the only ones here right now are Mrs. Charlotte McBride and her daughter, Matilda. Are they—"

"Apologies, ma'am, but we have reason to believe that Captain Bill Stuart is here as well. Can you show me which room is his?"

"I— But— Wait. How . . . ? Is this about the inn burning down?"

She shook her head, trying to seize upon a complete thought. Behind her, Edith heard the McBride women stand to join her at the door. The sheriff did not respond to any of her questions, but waited stoically.

"Right. Stuart." Edith turned to the McBrides and asked, "Did either of you see Bill Stuart today after breakfast? I am sure I saw him leave, and I have not seen nor heard him return."

While Mrs. McBride was shaking her head, her daughter spoke up.

"I didn't see anything, but I did hear footsteps at the end of the hall. Near his room, but then also near Daisy's room, so . . ."

"When was this, Miss?" the sheriff asked.

"When I came back from the post office. In the last hour. The house was quiet and I was looking for my mother. It sounded as though whoever I heard was trying to stay quiet, too."

The sheriff nodded briskly and turned back to Edith. "We got word from Abner Reed that Stuart was heard in the saloon today talking about leaving town. We believe it is possible that he will be trying to catch the eleven-o'clock train out of Laramie later tonight if we don't stop him. I need you to help me."

"So you think he's here packing? Goodness. The man didn't have very much. It's no wonder if I didn't hear him. If he leaves without paying his rent for the last month—"

"If you could just show us to his room, ma'am?" Sheriff Sands said firmly.

"Right. Yes. I'm so sorry."

She stepped aside and ushered the two men into the parlor.

"Come. Uh, this way. Upstairs."

Walking up the staircase in a daze, Edith almost could not believe what was happening. Even after her suspicions that she had taken to the sheriff only a couple weeks earlier, she still had never really thought that a person under her own roof would get up to anything requiring the law. Her mind was full of these possibilities, and she didn't realize they had reached the second floor until the sheriff touched her elbow gently.

"Ma'am," he whispered. "The room?"

"Yes. Goodness. All right."

Edith stepped out of the way and pointed toward the end of the hall. "His room is in the back of the house. The door on the left at the very end."

Without another word, Sheriff Sands and Deputy Inglis marched down to the end of the hall. The deputy kept one hand on his gun, but left it in the holster as he watched his boss carefully. The sheriff paused in front of the closed door and leaned in to listen. After a moment —Edith couldn't hear anything from where she was—he stood up straighter and pounded on the door.

"William Stuart?" he called in a booming voice.

Everyone waited. Edith realized she was holding her breath. She heard a tiny scuffle downstairs and looked down to see that Daisy had joined the McBride women in the parlor to watch what was happening.

"William Stuart, this is the sheriff. I can hear you in there."

He banged on the door again.

Waiting breathlessly, Edith could not tear her eyes away from what was happening. She should go downstairs; she should usher the other women into the dining room and out of the way. But she couldn't. This was her home, her business—her tenant accused, and whatever was about to happen in the next several minutes, could change everything for her.

Edith watched avidly.

"William Stuart, you are under arrest for the arson attack on the General Sherman Inn on July eleventh.

Please open the door. Things will be better for you if you come quietly."

"Like hell I will!" came the shout from the other side of the door.

Edith gasped.

Deputy Inglis glanced at her and said in a low voice, "Maybe you should go downstairs, ma'am."

But before she could do anything, the sheriff had rammed his shoulder against the closed door, forcing it open. Edith flinched. She'd need to find the money to replace the entire door—but that was a small matter compared to the horror of housing a criminal alongside her other upstanding tenants.

"Let go of me!" the man yelled.

The sheriff and deputy had darted into the room as soon as the door was clear. From where Edith stood she could only hear thuds, grunts, and crashing noises.

"Don't make this harder than it needs to be, Stuart," the sheriff said.

Edith recognized Bill's voice in the angry cries, but it only took a few moments for the two lawmen to subdue him. They squeezed through the doorway, dragging Bill Stuart between them. He saw Edith and glared wordlessly, refusing to put down his feet to be moved more efficiently. A long drag mark began down the hallway from the sole of one of his boots.

"Sorry about this, Mrs. Bennett," the sheriff said through a clenched jaw. "Seems this ruffian doesn't respect anyone else's property."

She could not come up with any kind of coherent response before the men were then dragging their prisoner down the stairs. The other women must have gotten out of the way, because she could only hear the deputy muttering instructions to Stuart. Hurrying to the bottom of the stairs after them, Edith was still in a state of shock that any of this had happened at all.

"What's going to happen?" Mrs. McBride asked, appearing beside her.

Edith glanced at the other woman, grateful that at least one of them had some sense still.

"Circuit judge. Few weeks from now," Deputy Inglis said, redoubling his grip on Stuart's arm. "He'll sit in jail until then."

"I didn't do it!" the man protested.

"Save it," the sheriff told him, before turning to Edith and the McBride women. "Can I count on you all to be available for the judge or lawyers if necessary? Will Mr. McBride assist in keeping this man behind bars?"

"Of course," Mrs. McBride said.

"Yes, thank you," Edith added. "Thank you so much."

The lawmen had dragged Bill Stuart out of the parlor, leaving a bit of a mess in their wake. The corner of one of the rugs had been pulled up completely, and the side table in the entry had been roughly pushed back some three or four feet. Edith could only imagine what the man's room upstairs looked like.

"Thank you again," she called after them, as they pulled their prisoner across the porch and down the steps.

Edith stood on her front porch, watching the sheriff and deputy lead Bill Stuart away, toward the jail, toward his fate. When they reached the main road, she turned back to the McBride women and Daisy. All three watched with expressions of the same shock that Edith herself still felt.

"Arson," she said. "*Arson!* I'm so sorry that your family had to deal with this."

"I need to find my husband," Mrs. McBride said, grabbing her hat from the rack. "Matilda, you stay here in case he comes back. He needs—*we* need—to talk to the insurance company."

In moments, she was out the door. Mattie returned to the settee in a state of awe and excitement about what they had just observed, and Daisy left for the kitchen, to continue preparations for supper.

Edith took a deep breath and closed the front door again, trying to return to the calm that had preceded the sheriff's visit.

She could not be more relieved that Bill Stuart—with his rudeness and bad attitude—was out of her house. The fact that he would be meeting the justice he deserved, after all he had done, was a wonderful step. Though she was a little nervous about having yet another vacant room in her boarding house, seeing that malefactor brought to justice and the town protected was well worth her individual concerns.

Trusting that Daisy had supper in hand, Edith made her way upstairs to start cleaning up yet one more mess that Bill Stuart had made.

CHAPTER THIRTY-FOUR

In all the years that she had been teaching, Lillian still felt the thrum of excitement and opportunity on the first day of school. Though she would be working in the same classroom where she had spent all of the previous year, before the students arrived she wanted to spend a day or two there cleaning, sorting, and rearranging things as necessary. She would have many returning students, and now that she knew better what they needed, she felt as though she could set up the room better for them.

She loved teaching. She loved her students. She loved the routine of walking to school early in the morning, with a muffin or hard-boiled egg tucked in her bag, being alone in the classroom to sweep and get ready for the day. There was a part of her that still wished she could continue teaching forever—but then, that would be a completely different life than the one she had chosen when she married Ned.

She did not regret her marriage at all; she just wished she could do both.

On the Friday before school was to begin, Lillian left home just after breakfast. Ned had left before her, and she had deliberately not reminded him where she was going. There was no need to put him in a bad mood before a long day at the hardware store.

"I'll be back before supper," Lillian said, as she packed a hard-boiled egg, folder full of lesson plans, two books on botany, and an extra shawl in her small hand luggage to take to the school room. "Probably before that, before Ned. But feel free to send for me if you need anything."

Mary Ann grinned at her, arms wrapped around a big mixing bowl as she whisked up the cream. "I'm not worried. I'm sure I'll be seeing you before that."

"All right . . ."

Lillian let her sister's somewhat enigmatic words lie, and headed out to the early September morning. The fall temperatures were creeping in. Soon she would need to wear a heavier coat to walk to school. The leaves of all the aspen and maple trees in their neighborhood would be turning brilliant shades of orange, yellow, and red. Over the year and a half that they'd been living in Juniper Falls, it seemed to Lillian that every season was the prettiest.

All thoughts of Ned's disappointment in her fell away. The warm, expectant thrill of a new school year lifted her mood and made her feel as though she were floating down the half-mile walk to the schoolhouse. She spent her morning washing all the windows, as well as the worn chalkboard at the front of the room. There was time to sweep and to wipe down the surfaces of all the desks lined up in neat rows throughout the room. She had just started pulling old paperwork from the drawers of her desk when the door to the classroom opened.

Looking up from her work, Lillian saw first her husband, and then her sister, enter.

"What are you two doing here?" she asked, only to be surprised by a third person following them into the classroom. "Silas? What on earth—"

She looked to her husband, but he seemed just as confused as she was.

He shrugged. "She's refused to say anything."

Coming around her desk to meet her guests in the aisle, Lillian looked back to her sister, who seemed to be full to bursting with excitement and who carried a picnic basket over one arm.

"Mary Ann?"

"Can we sit? I brought lunch."

"What—? I— All right . . ."

The hint of an idea floated into Lillian's mind, but she did not consider it too closely, preferring to let her sister reveal whatever she had come all the way to the schoolhouse to say. Both she and Ned sat uncomfortably in the small chairs, behind desks built for children, while Mary Ann put her picnic basket on the floor by Lillian's desk at the front of the room. Silas spread a flannel blanket over the top of the desk, on top of piles of paper and all.

"But—" Lillian made to stand up, to clear off her desk and get her things out of the way.

"It will be fine, Lil," her sister said. "Let me just—Trust me."

"All right . . . ?" She took her seat again and exchanged a confused look with Ned.

Silas still hadn't said anything, but he stepped up to Mary Ann's side and took her hand.

"Remember last week when Silas and I went to Laramie for the day?" Mary Ann began. She grinned widely and looked at her beau. "Remember how I came home and had such trouble sleeping that night?"

Ned and Lillian nodded.

"We haven't told anyone yet. We wanted you to be the first to know and to make it a whole special . . ." She waved at the picnic basket, blanket, and wider room. "It's a really special thing, and we wanted you to be part of it."

"Part of what, dear?" Lillian asked softly.

Mary Ann looked at Silas again. Without taking his eyes off her, he spoke for the first time.

"I have asked Mary Ann to marry me, and she said yes," he said proudly.

Both Lillian and Ned exclaimed happily, the former jumping to her feet to hug her sister. The story of Silas's proposal spilled out—a picnic on the ranch that Silas would be leasing—and Lillian noticed her sister could not stop looking at Silas. She seemed positively smitten.

"What's in the basket?" Ned asked.

Mary Ann blushed. "I wanted to celebrate. Something a little special."

She reached into the basket and pulled out a small stack of plates, utensils, and then, finally, a gorgeous, decadent cheesecake. It was plain, until Mary Ann then pulled out a jar of raspberry preserves. After slicing a generous piece for each of the four of them, she spooned a drizzle of preserves overtop, creating a treat fit to celebrate an upcoming wedding.

"I still need to spend another couple months getting the ranch ready," Silas said between bites.

"But we were thinking about getting married at the New Year," Mary Ann finished for him.

"We can move in and have time to get settled before it's time to put in the spring garden and crops and all," Silas added.

"Will your aunt and cousins be all right without you?" Ned asked. "Since your uncle died last year and all."

"Oh, yeah, Matt—my cousin Violet's husband—is taking to ranching like a duck to water. He would never say so, but I think he's looking forward to being the man in charge, and not feel like he has to run every decision by me just because I'm related. We brought on a new man earlier this year, and he's learning quickly too."

"We'll have to make sure your hope chest has everything you need," Lillian told her sister. "Start making a list tonight of everything we'll need to find before the end of the year to make your house a home."

"Thank you."

Mary Ann had tears in her eyes, and the two sisters shared a tender moment. Lillian reached out her hand, and her sister squeezed it softly. They didn't have to put words to thoughts to know what the other was thinking —how much they loved each other, how much they would miss living in the same house.

Ned broke the silence with another question about

the young couple's ranch, how far away it was, Silas's long-term prospects for expansion, while Lillian lapsed into silence to finish her slice of cheesecake.

Everything was changing. She had a decision to make.

The conversation continued, and Mary Ann and Silas lingered only until everyone had finished eating their slice of cheesecake. Once everything was packed away, the newly engaged pair said their goodbyes, insisting they did not want to take up more of Lillian's working time.

As she watched her sister and her newly betrothed walk away, she could not help but feel a sense of loss. Having her sister here on the frontier with her had been the biggest gift. She'd been able to feel at home in her new town so much more quickly simply because she had brought part of her home with her. She was broken-hearted over the thought of her sister leaving, but at the same time beyond thrilled for Mary Ann's future happiness.

She turned back to Ned, who had stayed behind.

They both knew there were things to talk about.

From the doorway of her classroom, Lillian looked at her husband, who remained on the other side of the room, half-sitting on her cluttered desktop. They held each other's gaze for a long moment, before Lillian took the initiative to close the space between them.

"I'm really happy for them," she said.

"I am too."

"And I think this solves our problem."

He frowned, confused, but she stepped into the space between his legs, leaning toward her husband and giving them a small, intimate moment without anyone else around. She felt his arms around her waist, holding her lovingly in a way she hadn't felt in weeks.

"Mary Ann getting married at the New Year gives us a timeline for me to leave teaching," she said softly.

He looked at her carefully, scrutinizing her expression for any hidden meaning. "Do you mean it?"

She nodded. "This will be the last year. I promise. The last semester. I can give the school trustees enough time to find my replacement, and then, once Mary Ann leaves our home, I will stay. I'll be happy being your homemaker, and hopefully we'll see our family grow."

"Lil—"

"But I need— Please. I just want to teach in whatever few months I have left before that happens. Please understand. It's just a short amount of time, and I want to say goodbye to teaching in my own way."

Ned opened his mouth as though to protest, but then just nodded before pulling her close in a hug.

"Of course," he said, his face nuzzled in her neck. "I want you to be happy. You know that, don't you?"

"Thank you. Teaching for a little while longer will make me happy. Seeing Mary Ann happily settled will make me happy. And I want you to be happy too."

"So . . . then you're right. I think we have our solution."

She kissed him and, when she pulled away again, studied his face. "Thank you for understanding."

"I'm trying. Thank you for trying with me."

He pulled her into another hug, and Lillian closed her eyes, appreciating the safety she felt in Ned's arms.

CHAPTER THIRTY-FIVE

Mattie stood with her parents in front of the newly finished hotel, waiting for them to be ready for their big announcement and official opening of the new hotel. She was glad she would not be asked to say anything; her attention was scattered, and she felt as though her thoughts were rolling about in her head like loose marbles. Just when she felt like she had a grasp on one, she managed to drop another.

Jack Kinsey stood in the back of the crowd that was slowly gathering around the newly hung, wide wooden double front doors of the hotel. He was deep in conversation with Daisy, Silas, and Mary Ann, and did not seem to have noticed Mattie at all.

Not that she needed him to, she reminded herself. Not that she *wanted* him to. She had a perfectly delightful beau in Philadelphia, and even though she had not gotten a letter from Duncan in several weeks, there was no doubt in Mattie's mind that he would come for her as soon as he could.

And she could always go to Jack Kinsey for horse-riding lessons. He'd shown himself to be a good friend.

In fact, Mattie wondered if Duncan and Jack might even find themselves to be friends one day. And then, maybe, whoever Jack married, Mattie could be friends with. They could be neighbors, and have each other over for supper, and—

Mattie shook her head, forcibly drawing herself out of her reverie.

She had plenty to worry about without making up scenarios involving people who were not here, or—in the case of Jack's imaginary wife—might not even exist.

She turned away from the crowd to look up at the hotel, to see what they all could see now.

It was truly remarkable how much work had been done in so short a time. Because her parents had tried to keep as much of the original structure as they could, there were still signs of charring and blackened bricks on the front of the building. Set as they were against the new molding, new glass windows, and newly painted wood trim, such darkened bricks only gave the structure more character. And Mattie suspected that, as the years went on, those scorched bricks would tell a story. As new visitors arrived to Juniper Falls, they would hear about how this hotel was literally built from the ashes.

Mattie was proud of her parents; she was proud of herself. And she was proud of this little town on the prairie, being so welcoming and so supportive of the McBrides.

Though she could admit to herself that she was not looking forward to the cleaning and maintenance duties of being the hotel's chambermaid . . . otherwise, she was very grateful with her life at the moment.

———

Lillian stood in the very back of the crowd, wanting to see the progress and all the work her friend's family had made without making Mattie feel as though she had to host her in any way. Her sister and Silas were a little bit closer to the hotel, but Lillian didn't want to interrupt their conversation.

The new school year had started the previous Monday, and with a whole week done already, she was preemptively mourning having to leave these children partway through the school year. When she had told Mary Ann about the plan she and Ned had made, the former promised to teach her all the recipes her husband liked, promised to make note of her regular schedule for cleaning and other chores around the house. Lillian wanted to slip into her new role as homemaker as smoothly as possible, and she hoped that the following few months of all the work at home would help distract her from the heartbreak of leaving her classroom.

She glanced over her shoulder to see that Ned was putting up his CLOSED sign and locking the door to the hardware store. He'd promised to attend this event with her, if only for a few minutes, recognizing that if a good portion of the town was at the party, not many would be looking to buy nails or rope or anything, and it would be good to mingle and socialize. He began crossing the street, smiling when he saw her watching.

"Didn't miss it, did I?" he said as he reached her.

"They look like they're going to start any minute. Mattie told me about the shortbread they've been baking all week. I wonder if it will be enough for this crowd, though."

"It's nice for your friend that there's so many people here, isn't it?"

"Yes, but it's too bad they already live here and have no need of a hotel room."

Ned chuckled and looked back up to the front of the rebuilt hotel. The clean glass front windows reflected the afternoon light and made the entire structure seem more open and luxurious than the previous General Sherman Inn had ever been.

"Well, we'll have to see what we can do. Maybe your family will want to come visit whenever the new Frye baby comes," he said in a low voice, looking over his shoulder to ensure he had not been overheard.

Lillian just grinned and nudged him. Mr. McBride was trying to get everyone's attention.

———

Edith had just left the sheriff's office in time to see the McBrides attracting a crowd in front of their hotel. After the sheriff had broken down one of her doors the week before, she'd been unable to rent out the room until the damage was repaired. But between gifts from the McBrides, various other neighbors who felt sorry for her, and the sheriff himself, Edith now held in her hand an envelope full of cash that should be enough to cover the repairs necessary. Though she still did not have a new tenant for that room—or the McBrides' or the

Watkinses' previous rooms—at least this would be one step in the right direction.

And there was no need to worry about such things now. She made her way to the crowd outside the hotel to watch and listen as the family made their big announcement. She and Daisy had been helping them prepare extra food for this very event over the previous couple of days. The kitchen in the hotel was finished, but still empty of the dishes, utensils, and any other tools useful to actually prepare food, so she was happy to offer her space to them.

Mrs. McBride had assured her that they would never forget how generous Edith had been to them, and promised that they would never treat her as a rival or danger to their own business.

And so, now that the hotel was about to be opened to guests, Edith let herself take the afternoon from chores to help them celebrate.

───────

Charlotte clasped her hands as they trembled. She was so nervous. She had not expected to be so *nervous*. Though this was the moment that she had anticipated and been looking forward to for weeks, now that it was here she felt excited and overwhelmed and hopeful and scared all at the same time.

It was here. The long ordeal was over. After all the work and investment they had put in to this new venture, finally the day had arrived that they could announce that their hotel was now open for business and christen it with its new name.

Henry must have seen her shaking, as he took her hand in both of his steady ones.

"Are you ready?" he whispered.

She beamed at him, unable to find the words for how happy and grateful she was for this day. Charlotte nodded.

Henry nodded back and turned to the small crowd gathered. There were far more people than Charlotte would have expected. Though they had made some friends during the month and a half they had been in Juniper Falls so far, she didn't expect so many of them to be so invested in their lives that they would come to what was really just a ceremonial event. Her eyes scanned the crowd and she picked out the Fryes, the Watkinses, the Langdons, the Harmons, and so many more.

"Thank you so much for joining us!" Henry boomed to those gathered.

They had crowded around the front door of the hotel, all along the boardwalk and spilling a little into the road. She looked over at all of them one last time before turning her attention to her husband. Henry held up his hat, waving it wildly above his head to call for everyone's attention.

"Ladies and gentlemen! On behalf of my family and myself, I would love to welcome you to the new Juniper Hotel."

He paused to put his hat back on as the crowd broke into cheering and applause.

"Please join us in the lobby for some light refreshments, as a thank-you for all the ways you have helped and supported us since we arrived in Juniper Falls. We are so proud for the McBrides to call you our new neighbors."

Standing to the side of the open double front doors, Charlotte watched in delight as all her new friends and neighbors filed into the lobby of the Juniper Hotel. Matilda had hurried inside to help serve the tea, cookies, and finger sandwiches they had prepared—with Mrs. Bennett's help—and Henry was shaking hands with every man who approached to congratulate them.

It had been a long, harrowing journey to this point, but Charlotte would not have exchanged it for anything. She and her husband were able to start their new chapter in a town where they could have a fresh start and a broad reach with this business.

Certain that this was one of the happiest moments of her life, Charlotte followed the crowd, entering the Juniper Hotel for the first time.

Thank you so much for reading *The Juniper Hotel*! I am so excited about this series, and so proud of this book in particular. It means the world to me that you are embarking on this journey with me.

I hope this to be the start of a big series, with multiple spin-off series. Your reading these books and reviewing and telling your friends about them would mean the world to me.

Some thoughts about this book...

Charlotte is the most like me of any character I've written. I too get overwhelmed and overstimulated—and you should see my stacks of yellow legal pads with scores of lists and notes to myself. For a character like her, leaving her home and routine in Philadelphia was likely very difficult. Giving her the stability in her relationship with a character like Henry is an important part of why she felt okay starting over.

Mattie was the most fun character to write. Though she's not based on any one person in particular, I have several friend like her, who are always up for something new while also being hard to pin down to set plans all the time. I hope you enjoy seeing her character grow the longer she is in Wyoming.

As part of the process of this novel, I researched how arson was investigated. Much of the tactics have now been debunked, but my characters in 1882 would not have known that. (I suggest listening to the podcast episode from Stuff You Should Know, titled 'The Dubious Science of Arson Investigation')

If you loved this book, there are currently more titles not part of this specific series that take place in Juniper Falls.

You can find a short story collection here: https://books2read.com/jfstories/

(This collection is FREE and includes the backstory of how Daisy found her way to town as well as how Mary Ann met Silas)

You can find a men's adventure here: https://book s2read.com/hawkesrevenge (which includes the story of the sheriff prior to Sands).

There is also romance series that takes place in Juniper Falls: https://atbutler.com/Sweet-series

Lots to read! And lots more to come! At the time of this publication, the first four books of this series are available to preorder here: https://atbutler.com/jf-series

. . .

And finally ...

A huge hug of gratitude to my friend Megan who just loves Victorian houses and so just happened to have a bunch of research and information about kitchens and cooking in the 1880s.

Thank you to my editor, Nerdy Wordsmith, for catching my slips and correcting timelines and encouraging me where the story is strongest. Any errors that remain are mine. Blame me.

And thank you to you, my reader, willing to take a chance on this new series. I would be nothing without readers like you.

A.T. Butler
August 2025

quick thinking, a touch of luck, and the kindness of strangers to reunite with their misplaced possessions.

Perfect for fans of historical fiction with heart and wit, this delightful tale reminds us that sometimes, the best memories come from the most unexpected mishaps.

DOWNLOAD Traveling to Juniper Falls for FREE here

———

Stories from Juniper Falls {FREE}

Juniper Falls Series:
    The Juniper Hotel
    Building the Dream
    Snowflakes and Sugar Cookies
    Prairie Storms
    Seeds of Change
    Golden Days

Marrying a Sweet Sister Series:
    The Sweetest Bond
    The Sweetest Spark
    The Sweetest Shelter
    The Sweetest Gamble

ALSO BY A.T. BUTLER

Stories from Juniper Falls

<u>Juniper Falls Series:</u>

The Juniper Hotel

Building the Dream

Snowflakes and Sugar Cookies

Prairie Storms

Seeds of Change

Golden Days

<u>Marrying a Sweet Sister Series:</u>

The Sweetest Bond

The Sweetest Spark

The Sweetest Shelter

The Sweetest Gamble

<u>Courage On The Oregon Trail Series:</u>

<u>Westward Courage</u>

<u>Faithful Trail</u>

<u>Frontier Sisters</u>

<u>Unyielding Heart</u>

<u>Wild Promise</u>

<u>Fierce Dreams</u>

Loyalty's Price

Riding for Justice

Trail of Redemption

Other Western Novels by A.T. Butler:

<u>Hawke's Revenge</u>

ABOUT THE AUTHOR

I grew up in the southwest—California Missions, snakes and constant threat of drought weaving the backdrop of my childhood.

But it wasn't until I moved to Texas a few years ago that the magic and mythology of the American West began to seep into my soul.

I'd love to write about western adventures, strong women and noble men for a long time.

If you enjoyed this book, a review on your favorite retailer would be greatly appreciated.

- A

www.ingramcontent.com/pod-product-compliance
Lightning Source LLC
Chambersburg PA
CBHW061652190726
48289CB00006B/1839